PRAISE FOR DAVID H. HENDRICKSON

"'Tiffany [Gets Her Boobs]' works beautifully, and by the end of the story, I had fallen in love with this savvy, determined, and somewhat crazy woman. Everyone who has read this story remembers it and likes it. You will too."

—*USA Today* bestselling author Kristine Kathryn Rusch

"I love ["Little Blue Fuzzy"]. David H. Hendrickson is one of my favorite writers. Use this piece as an introduction to his work."

—*USA Today* bestselling author Kristine Kathryn Rusch

"David H. Hendrickson tickles my funny bone in the best possible way."

—Annie Reed, author of *Pretty Little Horses*

"Good stuff... head-slapping, outrageous humor."

—Terry Hayman, author of *Chasing the Minotaur*

"One of the most diverse writers I have had the pleasure to meet.

—*USA Today* bestselling author Dean Wesley Smith

SHIMMERS AND LAUGHS

EIGHT WILDLY HILARIOUS TALES

DAVID H. HENDRICKSON

PENTUCKET PUBLISHING

COPYRIGHT INFORMATION

To Brenda, the Best Wife Ever.
Your support made all the difference.
Your love and laughter fill my life with joy.

CONTENTS

INTRODUCTION

From Female Impersonators to the Old Testament to Boob Jobs: The Genesis of These Stories

It all began for me with a friend lending me a short story collection by Harlan Ellison.

I'd always been a math-and-sciences guy in high school, and I'd spent those years with the tunnel-vision goal of getting into the Massachusetts Institute of Technology. After I got my acceptance letter—early decision, no less—I put about a half-second of thought into my future and decided I'd major in Electrical Engineering so I could design my own stereo system.

Yup. So I could design my own stereo system. That was my plan for the future.

Once I arrived at MIT, however, a much different reality hit me. It bashed me over the head like a baseball bat. All thoughts of listening to music on a stereo system I'd designed got tossed unceremoniously out the window. Crashing instead through my life's front door was the most mind-numbing, soul-crushing mathematics I'd ever encountered.

In course after course.

I don't hate math. In high school, I'd been co-captain of the math team. I'd thought algebra was fun and geometry pretty good. By the time the standard progression had moved to trigonometry and calculus, however, math had become drudgery. A necessary evil. I could appreciate their importance, but I found no fun in trig and calc.

At MIT, the next step led over the cliff edge of resigned acceptance into a deep, dark chasm of pure misery. Differential equations (diffy-q's in the parlance). Diffy-q's were a hundred times worse than the mathematics I had considered drudgery. A thousand times worse. A million.

I *loathed* differential equations. But they were an integral part of every engineering and math course, save Intro to Computer Programming, which used something called lambda calculus to suck the life out of that topic, too. Only a Music History course provided a respite from these assaults, and I was halfway prepared for that professor to use Diffy-q's to explain the wonder of Bach's *Brandenburg Concerto No. 2.*

I hated virtually everything about MIT and what I was studying. What I had considered my life's goal—to get into MIT and then somehow survive it, since I had known from the start that everyone else would most certainly be smarter than I was—had become a nightmare. I couldn't conceive of spending the rest of my life working on differential equations.

On top of that, I was working a few weeknights and Saturdays as a telemarketer for Sears Roebuck. If you bought any kind of appliance at Sears, I called to sell you a maintenance agreement that would cover all repairs and an annual checkup. And if you'd already bought a maintenance agreement at the store, I called to "up-sell" you additional years.

Yes, I was that guy. A creature below cockroaches. A telemarketer.

This made my work-school misery complete. Other than having found the most wonderful woman in the world (admittedly, the most important caveat possible), my life was a mess.

I was ripe for the plucking.

A friend at that part-time job always had a paperback book tucked in his back pocket. He also had a reputation for long bathroom breaks. It wasn't hard to put two and two together. The guy loved to read even to the point of skirting the precipice of getting fired.

One day, he lent me Harlan Ellison's short story collection *The Beast That Shouted Love at the Heart of the World*. It changed my life forever. I read the title story, the first one in the book, and it hit me square between the eyeballs. Took my breath away. Poleaxed me.

This was what I wanted to do with my life! I didn't understand what the heck Ellison was doing with this very experimental story, but oh my God, I wanted to do it. The next day, I took out of sheet of paper and began to scribble the first couple paragraphs of my first story. To steal a line from Ellison himself, it felt like lightning was shooting out of my fingertips.

This was absolutely what I wanted to do with my life!

I was horrible, of course. I had previously shown not even a hint of interest in writing "that fiction stuff." I had none of the skills, none of the knowledge, none of even the foundation of having read a lot of fiction myself. When I'd gone to the library, I'd checked out *The Boy Scientist* and incomprehensible books about neutrinos because they were presumably pieces to the puzzle that would get me into the Promised Land of MIT and the sure-to-be bright future that would follow.

So those first few paragraphs were predictably dreadful. When someone came up from behind me and asked, "What're you writing?" I dove on that sheet of paper, covering it up as if it were a grenade about to go off. I couldn't let anyone see the humiliating words I'd written.

But that didn't change the dizzying, intoxicating power of *creating something* that flooded over me. Yes, this was undoubtedly what I wanted to do with my life.

Unfortunately, there was that minor little problem of being horrible at it—other than that, Mrs. Lincoln, how did you like the play? Unlike a twelve-year-old who finds writing and in blissful ignorance of his ineptitude creates story after story, getting better while never being confronted by his lack of skills, I was old enough to know I was awful. I could look at Ellison's stories, and then look at my own pathetic attempts, and see they were universes apart. They had nothing in common.

Nothing.

I also had an extreme brain imbalance. We all have a creative side of our brains and an analytical side. My analytical side was powerful, developed—overdeveloped, in fact—by a lifetime's focus on math and science, analyzing everything from algebraic word problems to debugging computer programs. My analytical brain's cold, objective evaluation of my laughable writing attempts told my malnourished, emaciated creative brain that I had no talent and there was no hope of ever acquiring any.

When I wrote, my analytical brain would point to a paragraph I'd just written and slam on the brakes. Scoffing, it would tell me to fix this word and that word, then point me to the thesaurus for an alternate choice. I needed to rewrite the entire sentence. No, rewrite the entire paragraph.

Forget about trying to tell a story. Fix every last detail. Fix this. Fix that. No detail is too small.

Don't try to tell a *new* story. Your story ideas are dumb. Any new idea you come up with will be dumb so don't bother. Instead, try to rewrite that steaming mound of crap called your last story.

You really do suck. Do you really think anyone will ever want to read this crap? Do you really *want* anyone to read it? It's embarrassing. Do you realize how awful you are? You're a fraud, don't you know?

A *real* writer starts writing at an early age. A *real* writer doesn't substitute writing as a life's goal for one that goes horribly sour. A *real* writer loves writing from the start.

My creative brain had no chance.

Writing in that era before electronic publishing also provided no feedback mechanism to let the writer know he was making progress. If you're a golfer, you can see your scores go down. If you're a salesperson, you see your commissions rise. If you play competitive chess, you see wins and draws replace losses, and your rating rises. But with writing, until you're close to the Promised Land of actually selling your work, you send stories out and they come back with a form letter rejection.

It's hard to maintain belief that you'll ever sell a thing.

And if your analytical brain—the brain you trust because even after the debacle of MIT, it's putting food on your table as a software engineer—if it tells you that you suck, you will always suck, and you are wasting your precious time, it's hard to argue. Especially when those form letter rejections keep adding exclamation points to what your analytical brain is already telling you..

————

Sports writing kept me going. And then it held me back.

I've been a sports fan all my life. It's baked into my DNA. I try to set limits on how much time I put into it (and invest any saved time into writing), but I could no more entirely remove sports from my life than I could willingly sever every last appendage from my body.

After the "Dick and Jane" books and their successors, I continued to teach myself to read by poring over the sports pages of the *Portland Press Herald,* the newspaper of record in southern Maine. Eventually, I was squabbling with my brothers over who got to read the sports section first. At one point, two of us kept getting up five minutes earlier than the previous day, morning after morning, so we could stand first in line by the front door and wait for the paper boy.

Baked into my DNA.

At the age of seven or eight, watching on a small black-and-white TV, I became enthralled by an outstanding Princeton running back by the utterly awesome name of Cosmo Iacavazzi (pronounced Yahk-a-vah-zee). I couldn't repeat that name often enough.

Cosmo Iacavazzi. Cosmo Iacavazzi. Cosmo Iacavazzi. (Even now as I type it, I'm smiling like a fool.)

I was smitten. Smitten to the point that almost a decade later, Princeton was my number two school of choice, behind only MIT. All because a running back named Cosmo Iacavazzi had caught my eye.

I kid you not.

I was a nitwit, but a sport-crazed nitwit.

Years later, college hockey was added to the repertoire when my son, Ryan, began his life-long obsession with hockey. I had followed college hockey from a distance, but didn't dive deeply into it until he was a nine-year-old "Junior Chief," playing in the same arena as the UMass-Lowell Chiefs and going to almost all their games. Soon, I was firing off emails about UMass-Lowell hockey and its conference, Hockey East, on HOCKEY-L, an email discussion group used by fans in the days before websites.

When websites began to pop up, the founders of US College Hockey Online (uscho.com) saw my writing on HOCKEY-L, and asked me to write for them.

An audience? An audience for my writing? Are you kidding me?

It wasn't fiction, but my short stories were going nowhere—I couldn't give them away—and every time I tried a novel, I'd quit in frustration as soon as I made the mistake of reading the god-awful dreck I'd written.

At USCHO, real live people would read my words! I was so starved for any kind of writing success at all, so desperate to reach readers of any kind, that this amounted to a flagon of artistic water offered to a writer dying of thirst.

I pounced. The USCHO founders warned that despite their professional aspirations, there'd be no pay in the early years while everyone tried to figure out how to make money on the Internet.

I didn't care. Money? I was far more desperate to have *some* reason to believe that someone, somewhere wanted to read my words.

The plan was for me to split responsibilities for covering Hockey East, one of the four major conferences. The 1995–1996 season had just ended, so we would write feature stories throughout the off-season as a means of ramping up interest (and our internal organization) for the start of the season in October.

Bubbling over with enthusiasm, I poured all my abilities —hopeful that I actually had some—into my first college hockey feature story. I submitted it, and held my breath.

Bull's-eye.

The powers that be decided they weren't going to waste my talents—*I had talent! I had talent!*—sharing the Hockey East beat with another writer. He'd be shuffled to another opening, and the Hockey East gig was all mine.

It was what my writer's soul so desperately needed—a reason to believe—but it also came at a steep price. I had a day job as a software engineer, I also taught Computer Science two or three nights a week at Boston University and UMass-Lowell, and most importantly, I had two teenagers that meant the world to me.

I wasn't going to sacrifice my daughter, Nicole, and Ryan.

Something had to give. I decided that I would focus my writing energies on USCHO for this initial ramp-up off-season and then for the season itself. When the season ended, I'd flick the switch and return to writing short stories.

Sacrificing fiction writing for a year didn't feel like much of a sacrifice. After all, I was giving up something that didn't have any apparent worth. I hadn't sold a single story. The only one that had been accepted had been at a small magazine that paid in copies, and it had ceased publication before that story appeared. Besides, I wasn't giving up writing stories. I was just putting writing them on hold. A long-term plan of writing college hockey for six months, then short stories the next six, seemed the perfect compromise. Six off, six on.

I dove in that first year, and gave it all I had. When at

season's end the USCHO staff gathered in a private room at the Frozen Four, the others pointed at me and began chanting, "MVP! MVP! MVP!"

It was a gratifying end to a successful first season. I might not be able to write fiction worth a lick, but I'd found a home in sports writing.

The fiction actually had to stay on the shelf another full year, though, because, intoxicated with my USCHO success —*success! Can you believe it?*—I decided to spend that first off-season writing a college hockey book. The short stories would have to wait.

The book project filled me with enthusiasm—I was real writer!—and I suspect subconsciously I was in no hurry to return to the persistent failure of my short stories. By summer's end, the book landed me an agent—something that seemed a big deal at the time, but I just shake my head over it now—but the book did not sell. It had a limited shelf life, and no publisher could have put it out in time for it to be anything more than the equivalent of year-old lettuce.

The following off-season, I finally did return to short stories. It had been a two-year absence, but it felt like twenty-two years. Every fiction writing muscle had atrophied to nothing. My sports writing had improved my style. Although it would take some time to realize it, it had also improved my use of dialog. Each time I pared down a coach's rambling interview quotes into something effective that still sounded just like that coach and no one else, and identified him just as surely as a dialogue tag, taught me lessons important in fiction.

I had also been learning how to make people laugh and sometimes cry. And I'd acquired a bit of a voice, albeit with no instincts on how to use it in fiction. I'd also learned that deadlines were not to be missed, and if that meant flipping the bird to that hyper-critical analytical voice, then so be it.

But the fiction-specific writing muscles were gone. I wasn't quite back to square one with those first scribbled paragraphs following the Ellison-fueled inspiration. But it sure felt close.

I swore never again to miss an off-season of writing fiction.

Even so, I soon found that writing fiction only in the off-season wasn't getting it done. Sticking religiously to six months on and six months off, year after year, wasn't going to lead me to any kind of fiction success.

I was at a crossroads.

Not to be immodest, but I'd become a big fish in the small pond of college hockey. I was the first part-timer and the first Internet writer to be honored with the Hockey East Media Award. I'd also shared in the Scarlet Quill Award. After my photo was added next to my columns, fans recognized me everywhere.

One night at a Northeastern University game, the student fans, mindful of the fact that in my column I'd picked their team to lose the game, began to chant in singsong unison, "Daaa-ve! Daaa-ve! Dave Hendrickson! You suck!"

It doesn't get much better than having the entire end of an arena chant that you suck.

Another year, I thought Boston College, usually a powerhouse, would be sunk because its goaltender had undergone hip surgery. I picked the Eagles to finish eighth in Hockey East. When they instead won the national championship, BC coach Jerry York teased me from the podium in his introductory remarks, saying, "Not bad for a team that

Dave Hendrickson said was going to finish eighth in Hockey East."

Yet another year, before the start of a Hockey East championship semifinal, the LED Ribbon Banner that rings Boston Garden had a surprise for me. Where usually scores and advertisements appeared, moving round and round the display, this time a list of names was circling the arena. It was titled "The Legends of Hockey East." My name was one of them.

I tell these stories not to brag, but to illustrate the level of my accomplishments in college hockey. I'd become significant, and I was proud of my work. Damned proud!

But my fiction-writing dreams were slipping fast away.

In 2000, I had finally sold a humorous short story, "Yeah, But Can She Cook?" to an anthology called *Food and Other Enemies*. But I knew the editor, so that gave it a big asterisk in my mental tabulation of successes, even though I thought the story was pretty funny (and readers agreed, so it does appear in this collection). What's more, I kept the resulting twenty-five-dollar check for so long—perhaps becoming a bit like Gollum and struggling to part with it—that by the time I finally tried to cash it, the publisher had closed the checking account specific to that anthology. The check bounced. So technically, I was never paid.

So depending on how one maintains the scoreboard, I either had only one published short story* or none at all.

Definitely at a crossroads.

Someone suggested that I should stop torturing myself with fiction, where I seemed perpetually frustrated, and stick with what I was good at, namely sports writing. On the face of it, that was the only rational choice. It made no sense, based on the evidence to that point, to keep slamming my head against the wall of fiction. It promised to be awfully sweet if I would just stop.

What's more, I was getting painfully close to my fiftieth birthday. *The big five-oh.* And all I'd accomplished with my short stories was...if not nothing, zero, bupkis, then a microscopic number painfully close to that. A humiliating result best considered a skeleton in the closet. Slam that door, lock it, and throw the key away.

But fiction was my passion. It was why I had started writing in the first place. I might be getting close to fifty, but I wasn't dead yet.

———

Jeanne Cavelos and her *Odyssey Fantasy Writing Workshop* kept my fiction-writing hopes on life support. Kristine Kathryn Rusch and Dean Wesley Smith breathed life into it.

Facing that impending fiftieth birthday, I had a heart-to-heart talk with my wife, Brenda, truly the best person I have ever met, and the most astounding partner imaginable. Without her, you most assuredly would not be holding this book in your hands.

I had to find out for once and for all, I told her, if I was wasting my time. I didn't want to be haunted on my deathbed that I'd given up too soon on what (other than family) was my number-one passion. At the same time, though, how many years of humiliation did I need before I would accept the obvious, the near certainty that I simply *did...not...have...what...it...takes?*

I was almost fifty! Halfway dead!

I had to know.

I described for my wife a six-week, live-in workshop that a World Fantasy Award–winning editor named Jeanne

Cavelos runs each summer. I could apply, see if I got in, and maybe...

Brenda told me in no uncertain terms to go for it. That meant no vacation for us. All to keep this flickering dream alive.

It was astounding support at a time that made no sense at all.

After I was accepted to Odyssey, I then had to convince my day-job boss to give me six consecutive weeks off close to the release of a key project. I didn't quite have to say that I would leave if he didn't grant it, but the implication was clear. This was not negotiable. And no, if something went wrong, I would not be able to ride to the rescue.

Approval was finally granted, albeit grudgingly, so long as I put all the pieces into place to avoid that key project from blowing up in all our faces. I did that as best I could, and headed off to Odyssey.

There, I worked with Jeanne and several guest writers, including Robert J. Sawyer, Christopher Golden, and Jeff VanderMeer. I bombarded every single one of them, multiple times, with one plea.

"Tell me if I'm wasting my time. Don't tell me what you think I want to hear. Tell me the truth. If I don't have what it takes, please put me out of my misery."

All of them responded that I was most definitely not wasting my time. I had things I needed to work on, but I was actually getting close to breaking out. I should keep going.

Armed with the mantra *The only one who can stop me is me,* I attacked fiction with a newfound ferocity. There would be no more six months on, six months off. I would write short stories all year long no matter how difficult. By this time, my daughter had graduated college and my son was about to enter his final year, so they were no longer around the house, needing the constant attention of their dad. However, I still had the oft-demanding day job, teaching evenings during the Fall and Spring semesters, and writing for USCHO six months out of the year.

Didn't matter. That schedule wasn't going to stop me.

The only one who can stop me is me.

In the year following Odyssey, despite my schedule, I wrote fiction 365 out of 365 days.

The passion burned more than ever. I put into practice some of the technique lessons I'd learned at Odyssey. And when Dean Wesley Smith notified those of us on the Odyssey email list that he and Kris Rusch were offering an upcoming Master Class, I eagerly responded.

Dean asked about my writing, but he wasn't ready to accept me into the Master Class until I gave him the 365-for-365 statistic.

"That's the kind of writer we can work with."

He gave me a challenge, the Story-a-Week challenge, that I now give to aspiring writers who ask for suggestions. Every week, you write a new story and send it out to a market. No rewriting an old story. No writing something and then shoving it into a drawer to fix later. A new story, start to finish. Send it out.

It's brilliant in its simplicity. For me, a guy who had gotten mired in the quicksand of rewriting a single story over and over and over until I was finally deathly sick of it, the challenge was a new lease on my creative life. When I got to Sunday night and sent the story out, I felt as though a burden had been lifted off my shoulders.

On Monday, I could start something new! This would be fun and exciting! I didn't have to guilt myself into thinking that I should grind the old one into something better—a fallacy since I'd seen plenty of times when revision number twenty was simply a 360-degree return to where I'd been with revision thirteen.

Each time I started and finished a story, I learned how to be a better storyteller. And I was having *lots* more fun.

By the time I attended Kris and Dean's Master Class, I was well on my way. Those two weeks, the toughest two weeks of my life, forced that cranky old analytical brain to give way to the creative brain. The cranky old fool didn't go easily, but it finally went down. No more driving with the brakes on.

And though I had thought I'd never try novels again, an exercise in the Master Class gave birth to *Cracking the Ice*, my first novel and one published a few years later by WestSide Books.

Sadly, it was published dead, but that's another story for another time. This introduction, which has itself threatened to turn into what feels like novel length, needs to stick to short stories. And that discussion has almost hit its end.

When I first started writing all those years ago, I had three dreams. I dreamed that one day, one of my stories would receive a Best Story Award. I dreamed that one of them would be selected for a Year's Best anthology. And I dreamed that I would hold in my hands a collection of my own short stories.

Well, early this year, I received word that my story, "Death in the Serengeti" will be appearing in *Best American Mystery Stories 2018*, my personal favorite Year's Best anthology, one which I've been buying for two decades. It will be released this fall.

A couple months later, I learned that two of my stories were finalists for the Derringer Award, presented annually by the Short Fiction Mystery Society. "Death in the Serengeti" was one of five finalists in the Best Long Story category; "The Kids Keep Coming" was one of five Best Short Story finalists. In May, the Society announced that "Death in the Serengeti" had won. I'll be presented with the award at the World Mystery Convention in September.

And the most supportive wife in the universe will be there with me to share it.

While two out of three ain't bad, I'm greedy. In hockey terms, I've gone for the hat trick.

You're holding number three.

Three dreams fulfilled in one year. I'm glad I didn't quit when every piece of evidence suggested—no, demanded—that I'd be a fool if I didn't.

I am, of course, euphoric, and hope to share that joy with all of you.

But it also doesn't end here. There will be more stories, more collections, and more novels.

I ain't done yet. I have new dreams to chase.

June 24, 2018

LITTLE BLUE FUZZY

INTRODUCTION TO "LITTLE BLUE FUZZY"

Writers use different tricks to spark the imagination in unexpected ways. This story came out of a challenge among friends to write something inspired by a piece of spam. The email kind, not the meat.

That sounded like fun, and it was. A ton of fun.

All it took was the first page of my spam folder, and the first subject line my eyes locked on to.

"Unleash the monster in your pants," it read.

I needed nothing more. I was off to the races. I won't say the story totally wrote itself, but it came close. I can't remember one I had more fun writing. I laughed my ass off.

I submitted it to a Kris Rusch workshop I was attending. She suggested only a few minor tweaks to the story itself, but *hated* the title. And for good reason.

I had kept my Captain Literal hat on when completing the Spam Challenge. I'd used the subject line for my story title: "Unleash the Monster in Your Pants."

It had seemed like an eye-catching title at the time. I'd figured that if I saw it in a Table of Contents, no other story would have a chance. I'd have no choice but to read it first.

Not everyone, however, is as warped as I am. Many readers, perhaps even the majority, would stay away from the story just because of that title. It might be eye-catching, but it's eye-catching in all the wrong ways.

So the title became "Little Blue Fuzzy."

Many months later, I was overjoyed to see the title on the Recommended Reading List on Kris's blog (kriswrites.com).

"I love this story," she wrote. "I first saw it in a workshop under a different title. The story was funny then, and it's funny now. David H. Hendrickson is one of my favorite writers. Use this piece as an introduction to his work."

Wow.

I've used "David H. Hendrickson is one of my favorite writers" on almost everything I've written since. It'll probably appear inscribed on my tombstone.

But for now, let's focus on that last sentence. "Use this piece as an introduction to his work."

If the great Kris Rusch thinks this story should be your introduction to my work, how could I pick any other to lead off my first collection?

LITTLE BLUE FUZZY

Thinking he was clicking on his "Sent" email folder when the cursor was actually two lines lower, Mickey DeMarco opened his Spam and found his eyes drawn to one message.

Subject: Unleash the Monster In Your Pants!

Mickey grinned as he leaned back in his swivel chair. How could he not click on that one? It had a ring to it.

Plus, there was the sobering matter of last Saturday night's fiasco with Tina Wolchowski. Mickey still couldn't believe it had happened. Or rather, *hadn't* happened. Forty-one years old, still in the prime of his life, *born* with a boner, and ka-boom, out of nowhere, no lead in the pencil.

And with Tina Wolchowski. Inconceivable.

The next time with Tina—if there ever were a next time, please God let there be a next time—he sure as shit wanted to unleash a monster in his pants.

As his state-of-the-art music system switched from 50 Cent to Fergie, Mickey clicked on the message and...

A tiny image on the page flashed blue and went blank.

Mickey felt a stirring in his crotch, something *extra*

down there. His pants bulged. Something, though it sure wasn't the former Old Reliable, was bouncing inside his pants, slamming into the fabric, seeking release.

And using his balls as a fucking trampoline.

Mickey DeMarco stood up and unzipped his fly.

A furry blue streak shot out, caromed off his computer screen, flew up to the ceiling, and plummeted down onto his keyboard.

A tiny, furry, blue creature, looking like the TiVo animated character minus the antennae, spread its arms out wide.

"You called?"

Mickey took a few seconds to respond. "Who the hell are you?"

Barely two inches tall, the creature looked all around, as if puzzled. "I'm The Monster."

Mickey DeMarco peered closer. "You don't look like no monster to me."

Fuzzy scrunched up his face, bared his tiny teeth, and raised his matchstick arms in a menacing pose. He growled.

Mickey looked around the room for hidden cameras and a TV personality lurking in the shadows.

"You ain't no monster."

Fuzzy thrust out his chest. "Who says so?"

Mickey coiled his middle finger against his thumb and flicked the little fuzz-ball to the edge of the desk; he felt soft, more doughboy than monster.

"Hey!" Fuzzy teetered on the precipice, tiny arms wind-milling. "*Hey!*"

Mickey snatched him up and held him out in his palm for a closer look. "I think the word you was looking for was 'help!'"

Fuzzy put his hands on his hips. "It's not in our vocabulary."

"Whose vocabulary?"

"The Monster vocabulary." Fuzzy cocked his head sideways. "You're not too quick on the uptake, you know?"

Mickey thought about crushing the little wiseass, but decided against it. "Yeah, well you're not much of a monster. Only took me one little flick of the finger."

Fuzzy looked taken aback. "You caught me off guard. I thought you were my friend."

"Why'd you think that?"

Fuzzy looked at Mickey as if he were dumb as rocks. "Cause you unleashed me."

Mickey frowned. "Yeah, well, you wasn't what I was expecting. If I'd a-known…"

"What were you expecting? What's wrong with me?"

Mickey scratched himself. "Never mind."

"No, tell me."

"You don't wanna know."

"Yes, I do."

"Well, I was thinking that…that the monster in my pants would be like…you know, a real diamond-cutter."

"A diamond-cutter?"

Was the little shit being deliberately dense? "A boner! A four-hour, go-to-the-hospital, bang-her-all-night boner. Not a little blue ball of…whatever you're made of."

Fuzzy looked at him with total incomprehension. "What's a boner?"

Mickey stared back. "You really don't know?"

"Am I supposed to?"

The tiny figure waited expectantly.

When some time later Mickey finished his facts-of-life explanation, Fuzzy could only say, "You're kidding, right?"

———

STANDING in front of the bathroom mirror in just his boxers, Mickey DeMarco splashed cologne on his face and underarms.

"Hey, take it easy with that stuff," Fuzzy said, waving his arms wildly atop the sink.

"Women like it. Drives 'em wild."

"You're overdoing it."

"Listen to me, little man. I don't need no help from you when it comes to the ladies. You wouldn't know a pussy from a potato chip."

Fuzzy checked the notes he'd taken while Mickey explained the facts of life. "Would too."

Mickey splashed more cologne on his hands and lathered it on his inner thighs.

"Not down there!" Fuzzy lifted his hands to his throat, gagging. "I won't be able to breathe."

Mickey bent over until his eyes were only a foot from Fuzzy. "Listen, pal, you ain't going down there. Not now. Not ever. It kinda creeps me out you was there in the first place."

In a blur of bright blue, Fuzzy plummeted to the floor, rebounded, and shot up the opening between Mickey's boxers and his hairy leg. Hanging upside down, Fuzzy poked his tiny head out from the bottom of the shorts. "I can't leave you. We're a team."

Mickey swatted at his boxers as if a spider had crawled up into them, bouncing on the tips of his toes and yelping, only to shoot up an octave when he whacked himself in the balls.

After a time, Mickey's moans and curses subsided.

Fuzzy poked his head out. "Was that an orgasm?"

"Of course not."

He glanced at his notes. "Were you whacking off, also known as spanking the monkey—"

"No!"

"Why is it called *spanking the monkey*?"

"I wasn't spanking the monkey."

"Were you choking the chicken?"

Mickey's anger erupted. "I wasn't choking the chicken or spanking the monkey. I was trying to crush your furry fucking head!"

Fuzzy cocked his head. "Why are you so hostile? I'm only trying to help."

"I don't want your help."

Fuzzy smiled. "I'm The Monster In Your Pants. This is my home. I can't leave now."

Mickey slid the boxers off and dropped them, along with Fuzzy, into a pile. He pulled on another pair, this one with the logo of the New York Jets. But as soon as the elastic touched his waist, a blue streak shot up his leg again.

"You can't stop me," Fuzzy said, his head appearing at the bottom of the boxers. "I'm here to stay."

After a very long time, Mickey asked, "Where down there do you think you're going? 'Cause if you think you're getting near the jewels—"

"Eeew! Gross." Fuzzy wrinkled his nose. "Give me some credit." He pointed inside the shorts. "There's a satin loop here in the back. It has the size and brand name. Makes for a perfect hammock after I shrink a little." He winked. "And you know about shrinkage."

———

AN HOUR LATER, amidst Café Renaldo's soft buzz of conversation and clatter of silverware against plates, Mickey sipped his wine and tried to focus on the story Katharine Martignetti was telling, something about an English professor having a crush on a female student named Yeats. Mickey guessed it was supposed to be amusing so he smiled in what he thought were the appropriate places, but based on Katherine's reactions, his timing was off. He shoved a mouthful of pasta into his mouth and nodded expectantly.

She was attractive enough, he guessed, as forty-something women went—her ad on the dating website had been surprisingly accurate—but shit on a shingle, she expected him to think too much. Earnest discussions of global warming, politics, and then this story about the English professor. What was this, a first date or a fucking IQ test?

It was tough enough just keeping his mind off what lurked inside his pants. Every time he sat up straight, Fuzzy and his satin hammock dug into his tailbone, forcing him to slouch, a natural enough state for Mickey except that it reminded him once again of the little guy down there in his pants.

"Have you heard a single word I've said?"

Mickey blinked. "Yeah, sure, I was just...ah..."

Fire danced in Katherine Martignetti's eyes, reminding him of a parochial-school nun ready to wrap his knuckles with a ruler. In the silence, he could almost hear the light thwack-thwack against her palm.

The words slipped out like a fart. "See, I got this bulge in my shorts—"

No previous date of Mickey's had ever thrown water in his face. He'd figured that happened only in movies.

Until Katherine Martignetti.

———

Days later, in no mood for another first date with anyone short of Heidi Klum or Marissa Miller, Mickey got together with an old fuck buddy, Janine Brookmeyer. Further into her forties than he was, Janine was a bit chunky for his tastes, with a plain face and sad eyes, but not bad as fuck buddies went.

Within minutes of her stepping into his apartment, they'd gotten right down to business, almost racing to the bedroom. Her top off, she'd loosened his belt, unzipped his fly, and slid her hand down his pants.

Fuzzy shot out in a blue flash. He caromed off Janine's naked right breast just inside the nipple, crashed into the bedside lamp, and fell onto the nightstand beside the digital clock radio.

Janine shrieked and covered her breasts.

After shaking his head to clear the cobwebs, Fuzzy thrust his hand into the air, tiny index finger extended. "Fear not," he proclaimed, sounding like Underdog in the old cartoon series. "I'm here to save the day."

Janine fell silent. Wide-eyed, she turned to Mickey, who opened his mouth only to close it.

"Who..." Janine began, then faltered. "What..."

"I'm the Monster In Mickey's Pants! And are you going to be one satisfied customer tonight!" Fuzzy glanced around. "Or this afternoon. Whatever the case may be."

Glancing nervously about, Janine gathered her top and bra.

"Whatever you two need," Fuzzy continued, "I'm here to provide. If Mickey can't get it up—" Fuzzy flexed his muscles "—I'll hoist his petard." A confused look crossed his face. "Or whatever it's called." He flashed the broad, confident smile of a used-car salesman. "Your pleasure is guaranteed.

Your orgasms will be boundless. Our team is brimming with confidence."

Janine dashed to the bathroom, slammed the door, and locked it.

"What the hell do you think you're doing?" Mickey demanded.

"I can't sit idly by while your love life withers away," Fuzzy said. "I'm taking a proactive approach."

"My love life was fine, thank you very much, until you came along."

Fuzzy eyed him, head cocked.

"Okay," Mickey said. "Except for that one time."

Janine emerged from the bathroom fully clothed. Her thumb and index finger stroked her lips. "How long have you been talking to the...um, the *little guy*?"

Mickey fumbled for words.

Nodding warily, Janine headed for the front door, giving him a wide berth.

"Wait!" Fuzzy called. "Let me explain. Mickey sent for me after he couldn't get it up for Tina Wolchowski."

Janine stopped. "Tina?"

Fuzzy looked back and forth between Mickey and Janine. "He wanted a *monster* in his pants. To pleasure sexy bitches like you."

Janine snatched her purse off the floor and flew out the front door with only a hurried, wide-eyed glance back.

Fuzzy looked perplexed. "Did I say something wrong?"

———

MICKEY TOOK CHARGE. He strode to his dresser, a pair of scissors in hand, and slid out the top drawer.

"No more hammocks for you," he said.

With two snips, the satin label fell free in his palm. He reached for another pair of shorts.

A blue streak shot to the pile of underwear. Fuzzy pointed a finger. "I wouldn't do that if I were you."

Mustering his old swagger, Mickey asked, "Why? What're you gonna do?"

"I'll have to hang out somewhere else down there. Some place you might like a lot less."

Icicles slid up and down Mickey's spine. Then anger began to burn deep within. Mickey turned the scissors in his grasp and stabbed at Fuzzy. A blue flash shot off to the right as the scissors pierced several layers of boxers.

Fuzzy materialized on the drawer's edge. "What do you think you're doing?"

"Listen, this is important," Mickey said. "I got another date with Tina Wolchowski this weekend, and you're not gonna screw this one up."

"Last time with her you screwed up all by yourself."

"That's besides the point!" Mickey tried counting to ten, but stopped at three. "You're not gonna spook her like you spooked Janine. She ain't gonna see you. She ain't gonna hear you. 'Cause you ain't even gonna be there."

"I can't leave you."

"Oh, yes, you can, little man."

"I can't! I'm the Monster In Your Pants. That's who I am. It's where I have to be."

Mickey felt like plunging the scissors into his own neck.

"I won't say a word," Fuzzy said. "Trust me. You won't even know I'm there."

When Friday night came, Tina's short, black skirt showcased wonderfully tanned legs and the promise of more. Her girls jiggled all through dinner, a delicious preview of coming attractions. And on the ride to his apartment, her hands roamed all over him.

Inside his bedroom, Tina got down to a lacey black bra and panties. Mickey moved into her embrace, no problem with Old Reliable this time. No sirree. He had a diamond-cutter for sure, poking against the fabric of Tina's panties. Without a doubt, this time he'd unleashed a monster in his pants.

Mickey groaned. Why had that phrase popped into his head? As his shorts dropped to the floor and a flash of blue streaked to the dresser, he thought of Fuzzy looking on. Fuzzy, whose reaction to Mickey's birds-and-the-bees talk had been, "You're kidding, right?"

Old Reliable began to lose it.

Mickey kissed Tina on the lips and then, removing her bra, moved lower. But instead of seeing those bouncing, beautiful breasts with their large, hardening nipples, his mind's eye saw Fuzzy on top of the dresser, observing with clinical detachment, taking notes like a lab technician decked out in a white lab coat.

Old Reliable faded even more.

Mickey slid his hands inside Tina's panties and found that special spot. She arched her back and tilted her hips. Surefire lead in the pencil on any other day....

But Old Reliable was gone.

Mickey licked her nipples, trying to conceal his failure. He caressed her special spot. Tina was ready, in heat for chrissakes, but...

She didn't say it. Didn't have to. The look in her eyes said it all. *What's wrong?*

She sprang into action, turning her attentions on him, passionate attentions, attentions he would have given his left nut for on any other day. But on this day, Mickey couldn't stop thinking of Fuzzy in his white lab coat watching this failure, shaking his head while scribbling his notes.

After a few minutes, Tina stopped. She tilted her head back and rubbed what must have been a cramp out of her neck.

She didn't need to say a thing. The word she had to be thinking screamed through his own mind.

Again?

What could he say? Once was a fluke; it could happen to any guy. But twice? What was that? A trend? A problem? No, it was a fucking disaster. Surely no other man had problems *twice* performing with Tina Wolchowski.

"I'm sorry." Mickey shook his head. "I don't know what's wrong."

Tina looked at him for a very long time, as if he were some relic in a museum. "It's okay," she whispered.

Face flushed, she gathered her clothes.

———

MICKEY HAD ALWAYS FIGURED that spammers deserved only slow, painful deaths, but what choice did he have? He couldn't go on like this.

The Internet search took only a few minutes. He entered his credit card information, downloaded the spamming software and database of email accounts, and ran the setup program. After removing his pants and taking a digital photo of Fuzzy relaxing in his satin hammock, Mickey typed:

Subject: Unleash a monster in your pants!

The little furball wasn't a bad guy. He was charming in his own odd way. Mickey just didn't want him in his shorts anymore. Or anywhere else. He'd have to get rid of Fuzzy the same way he got him.

Maybe someone else could put up with the little guy. Soon, someone would get that chance.

Mickey attached the digital photo to the message and feeling only the tiniest sliver of guilt, clicked the mouse.

For a few minutes nothing happened.

Then a blue streak shot from his boxers, flew into his computer screen and disappeared with a loud pop, as if sucked in by a tornado.

Mickey stared at the monitor. He ran his hand over the label in his shorts, smooth and bereft of Fuzzy.

He was free!

Mickey felt Old Reliable growing in his pants. He might never get another chance with Katherine, Janine, and Tina, but there were plenty of other fish in the sea.

Idly he clicked on the Spam folder, prepared to delete all the messages. He wouldn't make that mistake again. But one line caught his attention.

Subject: Nearby Nymphos Want Your Body

Mickey smiled. Was this for real? He doubted it. But one little mouse click wouldn't hurt, would it?

THE FLOATER

INTRODUCTION TO "THE FLOATER"

I have a reputation for being a bit of a hypochondriac. Some of my family may even choke a bit on the phrase "a bit of."

I fully admit that I've frequently said to my wife as I've headed out for a run, "If I fall over dead, you were the Best Wife Ever. Love you. Make sure you always let the kids know that I loved them."

The first time she heard those words, they freaked her out. (What a surprise!) After a few hundred repetitions, however, her response became a nod of the head, a reassurance to me that she's sure I'm not going to croak, and I suggestion that I get going.

In my defense, I was born with an abnormal heart valve, a Bicuspid Aortic Value. I found out about it in my early thirties, and only started making morbid, hypochondriac remarks after doing misguided research about that valve. The first article that popped up in my search had an all too vividly memorable title.

"Sudden Death Syndrome in Bicuspid Aortic Valve Patients."

So I'm not a hypochondriac. I'm a chagrined reader of

journal articles best left to cardiologists. (And I'm certainly not as bad as the man buried in a Key West cemetery whose tombstone reads, "I told you I was sick.")

That said, I didn't have a tough time identifying with Hiram Silverman in this story. I really like Hiram, and I really like this story.

It was supposed to appear in a major anthology of humorous Jewish horror. A very nice payday was projected, and I was to share the Table of Contents with several illustrious names.

Sadly, it never happened.

Oy vey. I still love the story.

THE FLOATER

When Hiram Silverman first noticed the floater in his eye, he was sure it meant a brain tumor. He was sitting at the dining room table, three sips into his first cup of coffee and barely started on the front page of the *New York Times*. There it was, no matter where he looked—right, left, up, down, or straight ahead—a wavy thread in his vision all but screaming *inoperable*.

The floater underlined each word in the *Times*. It superimposed itself on the pepper shaker just beneath the two p's. In whatever square of the checked tablecloth he focused on, the black thread hung like the first strand of a spider's new web.

Hiram, short and pudgy with bifocals sliding down his broad nose, looked at the wall clock. The thread dangled just below the number twelve. He rotated his vision clockwise, circumnavigating the numbers. He then reversed direction and went counterclockwise.

"Will you look at that," Hiram said to Ruthie, his wife of forty-seven years. She died six months ago and never blessed him with an appearance as a ghost, but he never stopped talking to her. "I'm finished," he said. "*Kaput*."

Hiram tottered to the phone and dialed a number he knew by heart.

———

QUACK NUMBER TWO, Dr. Samuel Glick, extended his hand. Not to be confused with Hiram's *real* doctor, Quack Number One, Samuel had been Hiram's optometrist and off-and-on poker buddy for the past twenty-seven years. Tall and thin with salt-and-pepper hair, he wore a white lab coat over a blue shirt and striped tie. "How's my favorite old buzzard doing?"

"I'm dying," Hiram said.

"That's the spirit!"

Fifteen minutes later, Samuel set aside his instruments and handed Hiram a tissue to dab his watering eyes.

"In your left eye, you have what's called a floater," Samuel said. "Very common in people your age. Common and completely harmless. In fact, you're very lucky you haven't noticed one until now."

Harmless. No brain tumor. Hiram breathed a sigh of relief. He hated that phrase, *people your age*, but still...harmless.

Samuel handed Hiram his glasses. "Our eyes are encased in a gel-like fluid. But as we age, that gel breaks down. Its consistency deteriorates and the tiniest of black dots appear in our vision. Most of the time, you don't even notice. Larger ones like yours may be visible for a while, but often the brain cancels it out, stops processing its information. In essence, you stop seeing it. The brain is a marvelous thing."

Samuel straightened his instruments. "You've had floaters since you were in your late forties, but you didn't notice them because they were too small or in the wrong position."

"What?" Hiram said. "I've had these things...these floaters for all these years and never known about it? You never told me? *I should have been told!*"

Samuel glanced to the ceiling as if requesting help from on high. "Hiram, how long have you been coming here?"

"Your children, their college diplomas should have stamped on them, 'Paid for by Hiram Silverman.'"

"The point is that I know you, Hiram. I didn't tell you about them because they're completely normal. Almost everyone has them in some form by middle age. You've had hundreds of them without even knowing it. There's no need to alarm your inner hypochondriac."

"Hundreds!" Hiram shuddered. "Hundreds, you say? And for years?"

Samuel nodded. "But completely harmless."

Hiram glowered. "Did you call me a hypochondriac?"

Samuel pulled a ten-dollar bill out of his wallet and laid it on the table before him. "Ten dollars says you were convinced it was a brain tumor." He pulled another bill out of his wallet. "Twenty."

Hiram glared at the smirk on Samuel's face. "Put your money away, you quack."

———

So what if *the fluid in my eyes is breaking down,* Hiram told himself when he got back to his apartment. That should be a surprise? He didn't need an article in the *Times* to tell him his body was falling apart. If he could make it through the night with only one trip to the bathroom, it was a cause for celebration. If he could manage a daily bowel movement without a stick of dynamite up his *tuchis*, it was an occasion for a *b'rachah*. And for a decade or so prior to Ruth's death, if he could crank up an erection without the aid of cantilevers, support beams, and flying buttresses, not to mention little blue pills, it was equally miraculous.

He was old. Seventy-five years old, to be exact. To quote Louie from 23B who fancied himself quite the comedian—he should be in show business, he was so funny—Hiram didn't look a day over eighty. But it rankled Hiram to be reminded of it wherever he looked. The wavy thread felt like a skull and crossbones superimposed on every image.

"I curse you!" Hiram said, waving a wrinkled and liver-spotted hand. "*Gay avek!*"

A sense of foreboding came over him. Unless his imagination was playing tricks with him, the floater had just gotten bigger.

———

By the following morning, Tuesday, the floater had grown from a thin thread into a round splotch about the size of a lower case character in the *Times*' newsprint.

"The brain may cancel it," Hiram said, shaking his head as he recalled Samuel's words. "What a quack."

Still in his bathrobe and slippers, he poured his coffee, stirred in sweetener—sugar had become verboten after the onset of Type 2 diabetes—and took a sip. He frowned. He took another sip. Its aroma wafted up his nostrils every bit as strong as always, but there was no taste to it at all.

He stirred in more sweetener.

Still, nothing. It was like drinking hot, black water.

His first instinct was to call Samuel. But Quack Number Two, who was only an optometrist and not a real doctor on par with Quack Number One, had called him a hypochondriac. Hiram was loath to give him more evidence just one day later. Hypochondria? He'd give Samuel Glick hypochondria right between the eyeballs.

Hiram trundled back to the kitchen, *Times* in hand. After inserting bread in the toaster, he checked the coffee maker and started over.

Hiram flipped open the paper. He tried to concentrate on an article about famine in Central Africa, but the *heslekh* floater distracted him from every word. He read a sentence once, twice, and then a third and fourth time, getting to the end without any idea of what he had just read. The little black blob was everywhere.

He carried his toast and fresh cup of coffee into the dining room. He blew on the steaming coffee and took a sip.

"What the—"

He couldn't taste it at all. Hiram bit into the toast. It was like eating cardboard.

"Ruthie, the quacks have ruined my life," Hiram said. "No butter; margarine. No cream in the coffee; skim milk. No sugar; artificial sweeteners. No wonder I can't taste the *fecockteh* thing."

He trundled back to the kitchen, poured yet another cup of coffee, but this time stirred in sugar out of the secret bowl in the back of the cupboard. On a fresh piece of toast, Hiram smeared butter, not margarine, and wasn't bashful about it. He slathered it on just like the old days.

It made no difference. There wasn't even the hint of taste.

"*Oy Gevalt!*"

Later, after closing his eyes and listening to Benny

Goodman and Duke Ellington for a while, Hiram walked to the deli a block and a half away. His hip hurt and so did his knee, but the trip was always worth the trouble.

He ordered his favorite, a hot pastrami sandwich on rye. Their pastrami was to die for, succulent, with all the juices trapped inside the bread, and who cared if Quack Number One said it was bad for his cholesterol. A man had to live, didn't he? If you couldn't enjoy a hot pastrami sandwich every now and then, what was the point?

Except this time Hiram didn't enjoy the pastrami at all. Its smells were as tantalizing as ever, but his eyes widened as he took one bite and then, feverishly, another and another.

Nothing.

The juices rolled over his tongue, but they might as well have been drops of tap water.

———

BY WEDNESDAY MORNING, the floater had grown to the shape of a clenched fist, almost twice the size of the *Times* newsprint. It was now all but impossible to read. Hiram tried cocking his head and looking out of the corner of his eyes, like a robin searching for worms, but the clenched fist tracked wherever he focused, obscuring every word. If he looked below the intended line, the floater shifted beneath it only to bob up and superimpose itself on top of the text when he tried to peek at the words.

It took every ounce of Hiram's restraint for him to stay away from Quack Number One. Only one thing stopped him. Anyone with an inner hypochondriac knew that every last self-respecting doctor spent Wednesdays on the golf course, leaving the ill and afflicted, not to mention those with inner hypochondriacs in full bloom, to youngsters possessing all the experience of a babe fresh out of the womb. Unless you wanted to die a horrible and agonizing death at the hands of a rookie, you didn't even think about going to a doctor's office on a Wednesday.

"Tomorrow," Hiram said. "As soon as they unlock the doors."

And it was time, he told himself, today, right this instant, for him to abandon this cockamamie idea of his brain doing anything to rid him of this floater. Samuel had given him hope—*often the brain cancels it out, stops processing its information*, he had said—but Hiram didn't think of Samuel as Quack Number Two for nothing.

Determined to read the *Times*, Hiram closed his offending left eye and watched with glee as the clenched fist vanished.

"*Meisseh Meshina!*" he cried. *May you die a horrible death.* Hiram could see again.

He read about an earthquake in China. And then an analysis of the HIV death toll in Africa. And the latest Washington infighting over the federal budget.

"*Oy!* Who wants to read this dreck?"

Hiram turned to the editorials and read about the latest twist in the Palestinian conflict. And Iran's nuclear program. And global warming.

"Enough already!" Hiram said.

Midway into an article on a new threat to the Everglades, the floater returned, first in just the corner of his eye, as if peeking from around a corner, and then springing into full view. Its fist shook, as if with anger.

Hiram groaned. He opened his left eye, briefly saw double—two shaking fists—and then the two images converged.

Hiram crumpled the paper and threw it down. He hobbled out of the apartment, slamming the front door.

He pounded on the elevator button. When it didn't instantly open, he muttered, "I'm not getting any younger!"

Finally, the elevator door opened. Hiram hit the lobby button and then pressed "Door Close" repeatedly.

When the elevator stopped on the next floor, Hiram stared at the lighted number eight, the floater's fist superimposed on it. Mrs. Sipowicz and her omnipresent cloud of perfume clambered on.

Except that, even as he began reflexively to hold his breath to avoid inhaling the cloying fumes, which he was convinced were carcinogenic, Hiram realized that Mrs. Sipowicz's cloud was missing. Hiram sniffed as discretely as he could.

Nothing.

When the elevator reached the lobby, Hiram pressed the button for his floor and rode back up to his apartment. There was no escaping the floater.

He could all but hear it laugh as it shook its fist.

———

When Hiram opened his eyes on Thursday, the floater flipped him the bird. Staring at the ceiling, Hiram watched as the fist rotated and extended its middle finger.

Hiram faced the digital clock on the nightstand. The finger obscured two of the three red digits in the display.

He fumbled for his glasses. He looked at the calendar on the far wall, still showing March, the month of Ruth's death. He focused on the square for the eighteenth, a Thursday. From just below the right corner, the middle finger pulsed.

Hiram lumbered to the phone mounted on the dining

room wall. Quack Number One or Quack Number Two? Hiram flipped through Ruth's phone book, barely able to make out the numbers.

With the finger superimposing itself upon whatever touch tone key he looked at, Hiram pounded out from memory the sequence of Samuel's phone number, grinding the tip of his finger against each key as if he could crush the vulgar image like an offending bug.

An answering machine came on. Hiram looked at the clock, cocking his head enough to make out that the office wouldn't be open for another half hour.

Hiram put the phone down and closed his eyes. He counted to one hundred before opening them. The middle finger still flashed its vulgar message: *Up yours, old-timer!*

Hiram put the coffee on, purely out of habit, lumbered to the bathroom, and climbed into the shower.

Minutes later, deep in thought, he glanced down and saw the skin on his chest and thighs had turned scarlet.

The shower's knob was in the high noon, scalding-hot position. Hiram dialed it back to three o'clock and turned away. He must have hit the knob with his elbow.

He put his hand out. The water felt neither hot nor cold. Hiram turned the knob clockwise to nine o'clock, an ice cold position that normally would have set off shivering and yelping, but he felt nothing. Even with soap still on his arms, he turned the water off.

Temperature, Hiram thought. Taste, smell, and now temperature.

Gingerly, he patted himself dry. After putting on his bathrobe, he went to the kitchen and poured a cup of coffee. Steam rose into the air.

On Tuesday, it had tasted like hot water, albeit with the familiar aroma that helped waken his senses each morning.

Yesterday, it had lost its aroma. Today, he couldn't distinguish it from water at room temperature.

Hiram punched in the number for Samuel's office. This time, the receptionist answered.

"This is Hiram Silverman," he said. "I have a terrible emergency. I must see Dr. Samuel immediately."

Silence fell on the phone line.

"Hello?" Hiram said.

"I'm here, Mr. Silverman," said the icy female voice. "But you had an emergency on Monday, too. Dr. Samuel is extremely busy today."

"Listen, you," Hiram said, his hands shaking. "I've been seeing Samuel since before you were even born. Don't tell me that he's too busy to see *me*. I have a serious medical emergency."

"Perhaps you should go to the hospital," the Ice Maiden replied. "If you have an emergency, I can call you an ambulance. What is the problem?"

"I need to see Samuel!" Trembling, he shouted, "Put Samuel on the phone or I'll...sue you back to the Stone Age!" For the next few seconds, Hiram heard only the furious pounding of his heart.

"One minute, please."

Samuel came on the phone. "Hiram, what's the problem?"

"The floater. It keeps growing and...I'm not being a hypochondriac. It's...it's huge now and it's...you're not going to believe this, but it's giving me the finger."

"Hiram, slow down," Samuel said, a mix of concern and confusion in his voice. "You're not making any sense."

"It's giving me the finger!"

"What finger?"

"*The* finger, you *putz*! Listen to me. Yesterday, the floater was a fist. Bigger than the letters in the newspaper. Today, it formed itself into a middle finger sticking up at me. The floater is giving me the finger."

Silence.

"Samuel, are you still there?"

"I'm here, Hiram."

"I'm not making this up."

"Come over right away," Samuel said. "If you're not here in forty-five minutes, I'm calling an ambulance."

THE FLOATER FLIPPED the bird at Hiram while he got dressed, during the ride in the taxi, and in the waiting room. When he glanced at the glowering Ice Maiden, the finger blocked out her pursed lips. When he looked at the rows of glasses frames mounted on the walls, the finger looked out from each right lens.

Samuel poked his head out from the exam room. The floater flashed its extended middle finger in exuberant pulses of red and purple on Samuel's forehead.

"Hiram!" he said, and strode toward him, a grave look on his face.

The floater's aura intensified, pulsating in kaleidoscopic patterns that rotated with dizzying speed, flipping Hiram the bird upside down, sideways, and at every angle in between, flashing its vulgarity in pastels and then shades of neon until returning to basic black. Hiram could barely detect the open exam room door.

And then as Hiram crossed over the threshold into the exam room, the middle finger closed back into a fist. The fist collapsed into itself. It withered away like a punctured balloon, leaving behind only the mere cobweb thread of three days ago.

Hiram stopped dead in his tracks. His lips became dry. His hands shook.

"Hiram, are you all right?" Samuel put a hand on Hiram's shoulder. "You look terrible."

Where was the middle finger? Where was the clenched fist?

"Hiram? *Hiram?*" To the Ice Maiden, Samuel said, "Call an ambulance!"

Hiram touched him on the elbow. "No. I'm all right."

"Give me one good reason not to rush you to the hospital."

Hating himself, Hiram said, "Because it's me." He felt his shoulders slump.

Samuel looked at him closely. For a time, he didn't say a word. "Are you sure?"

Hiram nodded.

Samuel waved off the request and led Hiram into the examination room. "Talk to me."

Hiram spread his shaking hands wide, uncertain of what to say.

Samuel leaned close. "What's this about the floater... giving you the finger?"

Hiram looked up, down, and to both sides. Only the original thin thread, barely visible, remained.

"It went away," Hiram said in barely more than a whisper. "Forget it. I'm sorry I bothered you."

"What?"

Hiram got up to go. "Just have the *chaleria* call me a cab. It...the finger went away."

A look of anger flitted across Samuel's face. "Hiram, I rescheduled appointments to accommodate you. You sounded *terrified*. I almost sent you directly to the emergency room and I know how you hate hospitals. But now you tell me to just forget it?"

Hiram rubbed his temples. "I guess I am just a hypochondriac."

"That's news?"

Hiram shook his head and shrugged. "I don't know what's happening to me. On the other side of that door, I could barely see. The floater was so huge and giving me the finger.... But then I stepped in here and...it's gone."

Samuel's brow furrowed. "Let's take a look." He took Hiram's vital signs and then repeated Monday's examination.

"Your eyes haven't changed," Samuel said. "Of course, it has been only three days."

Humiliated, Hiram remained silent. He had planned to mention his lost senses, but not now.

"As for this giant floater giving you the finger..." Samuel took a deep breath. "That's probably a manifestation of your anxiety. I'm going to use a word now and I'll probably regret it because you'll latch onto it like you did with *hypochondriac* and like you've done with other words I've used over the years. But I'm going to use a word you won't like. Psychosomatic. I believe your brain, distressed over the appearance of the floater and...let's face it, Ruth died only a few months ago."

"Six." Hiram drew in a deep breath. "Six months, seventeen days, and..." He glanced at his watch. "Three hours and fifty-two minutes."

Samuel nodded. "That was a horrible shock to your system. So in all likelihood, anxiety has triggered this illusion of a middle finger. That doesn't make it seem any less real. It's very real to you. It doesn't mean you're crazy. It doesn't mean you're senile.

"But I'll take no chances. I'm going to call an ambulance and have you taken to the emergency room."

"No!" Hiram trembled. Hospitals were where people went to die. "You're right about the anxiety. I'm sure of it. That's all it is. I'm as strong as an ox."

"Strong as an ox?" Samuel snorted. "You're as bull-headed as a mule." He stared at Hiram for a long time. "Any other patient would be in that ambulance even if I had to put him in restraints myself. But your vital signs are fine and we have been down a few of these roads before, haven't we?"

Hiram nodded.

"More than a few times."

Eyes downcast, Hiram continued nodding.

"Okay, then," Samuel said. "No hospital. But I'll have my office coordinate with your primary physician for a complete physical with blood work and a brain scan and whatever other tests they feel would be appropriate. At his office, not a hospital."

"Thank you, Samuel."

Samuel pointed a finger at him. "And if anything, I mean anything, makes you feel the least bit funny, you had better call yourself an ambulance, or at least call me. If you don't, I'll come to your apartment and beat your thick skull with a baseball bat. Do you understand?"

Hiram, mouth dry, nodded.

They shook hands and Hiram hobbled out of the examination room and past the Ice Maiden.

As soon as Hiram closed the office door behind him, the clenched fist reappeared and the middle finger extended, even larger than before and pulsing with enthusiasm.

Maybe it is a brain tumor after all, Hiram thought. But he doubted he was so lucky.

————

ON FRIDAY, Hiram was partway into one of his monologues with Ruth when he realized that he couldn't hear a single word.

"Ruthie?" Hiram said.

Nothing.

He turned on the TV set, cranking the volume up.

Nothing.

He turned on the stereo and put *Stomping at the Savoy* on the turntable.

Nothing, not even the hiss and crackle that always told him it was real music on real vinyl, not the antiseptic digital dreck that passed for music these days.

"I have no choice," he said, his words silent as if spoken in a vacuum.

The middle finger flashed with exuberance.

Hiram picked up the phone, about to dial 911, but got no dial tone.

He shook his head, one part amused and the rest of the parts horrified that he'd not only expected a dial tone but that he'd be able to summons an ambulance without being able to hear a thing. He really was losing his mind, wasn't he?

Hiram took the elevator down to the lobby and asked the doorman to call 911.

"This is it," he said, knowing from the reaction of those around him that he'd been audible to everyone but himself.

————

Samuel arrived at Hiram's single room in the hospital late that afternoon. Using a black marker on a clipboard-sized whiteboard, he wrote: *I came as fast as I could. Laser surgeries.*

Hiram cocked his head every which way to make out the words, one letter at a time. He nodded.

What happened?

Hiram erased Samuel's words and scribbled a barely legible reply.

Losing my senses. Taste first then smell and temperature. Today, hearing.

Samuel nodded and pointed to the pad, asking for it. Hiram held up an index finger and wrote.

The floater is blocking my senses.

Samuel took the pad.

I can't believe that. We'll find the real problem.

Hiram shook his head. *It's the floater.*

———

On Saturday, the floater blocked Hiram's sense of touch. With it went almost all semblance of communication. The huge middle finger now occluded over half his field of view.

Why me? Hiram wondered. Had he been such a bad person? He wasn't perfect, he knew, but who was? Maybe, he thought, there was no moral explanation at all. He didn't need the *Times* in front of him with its endless tales of misery to know that cruelty often picked its victims randomly.

But perhaps, Hiram thought, he'd brought this all upon himself by cursing the floater what now felt like a lifetime ago. Maybe the vile thing had been nothing more than what Samuel had said, broken-down gel. Harmless. Until, that is, the curse had awoken something best left alone.

Or, Hiram wondered, was he the world's most exceptional hypochondriac, able to conjure all of this out of his own mind? Which led to an even more terrifying question. Why would his own mind try to destroy him?

———

SAMUEL ARRIVED SHORTLY AFTER NOON.

Hang on, you miserable old coot, he wrote, tears welling in his eyes. *We'll figure this out.*

It took Hiram minutes to decipher the message.

Hiram flopped a useless hand toward his eyes.

Samuel scribbled on the pad. *The floater?*

Hiram nodded vigorously.

Samuel closed his eyes as if in prayer.

After a time he wrote again on the pad. *Your daughters have been notified. They're flying in.*

———

ON SUNDAY, the floater blocked Hiram's sense of pain. Nurses prodded him with needles, first near the fingertips, then the backs of his hands and his arms, and finally his legs and feet.

He felt nothing.

His daughters arrived, Miriam accompanied by her husband and Sarah alone. In case the floater was contagious, Hiram motioned them to the foot of his bed but no closer, not even the son-in-law.

When his daughters blew him kisses, gestures that he made out only after cocking his head back and forth and up and down, Hiram held both palms to his heart.

———

On the eighth day, the floater, left with no further senses to destroy, ballooned larger and larger like a tick so bloated with blood it looked ready to explode. Pulsating with metronomic regularity, it covered all but the peripheral edges of his vision.

Hiram assumed the four shapes at the foot of his bed were Miriam, Sarah, Michael his son-in-law, and Samuel. For a long time, they appeared to huddle, arms around each other, heads bent.

"I should have spent more time with the girls," Hiram said to Ruthie, though he couldn't hear the sound of his own words. "But maybe it's better this way. Easier. They won't miss me so much."

And as that thought struck him like a clenched fist, he asked, "Have you missed me, Ruthie? Have you missed me at all?"

———

The floater lowered its finger. The fist rotated, turning its palm out and wiggling all its fingers.

Hiram thought he heard Ruthie's voice calling him.

The floater waved goodbye.

YEAH, BUT CAN
SHE COOK?

INTRODUCTION TO "YEAH, BUT CAN SHE COOK?"

This is my first published story. As such, it bears a few warts and blemishes that I'd like to believe my newer pieces do not.

I didn't try to remove all those blemishes. At a certain point, a story becomes a new one if too many changes are made, and I didn't want that. I made more wording changes than I anticipated because tweaks become natural and instinctive while fixing errors in the conversion of the scanned story. What remains, however, is 99-percent identical to the original.

Warts and all, "Yeah, But Can She Cook?" is a funny story that will make you laugh. And more than a few of us will identify with Stuart Rumpleman's love for food.

YEAH, BUT CAN SHE COOK?

Stuart Rumpleman looked at his plate and wanted to cry. He should be savoring a two-inch-thick sirloin steak, lightly charred on the outside but still pink in the middle. Or a slice of prime rib awash in its juices. Or a simple bacon, lettuce, and tomato sandwich, smothered in mayonnaise, heavy on the bacon. He should be digging into a mound of fried clams, shrimp, and scallops. Or devouring a turkey drumstick, leg of lamb, or southern-fried chicken breast. At the very least, he should be squeezing a lemon slice over a nice pound of fish, that healthiest member of the meat food group.

What he wouldn't give right now for a piece of haddock, flounder, or swordfish. Or if he could really have his pick of the aquatic litter, he'd go for the sautéed Florida pompano that he'd devoured at a place called the Reef Grill while vacationing in West Palm Beach. Or dolphin, which he'd called mahi-mahi ever since a blind date confused it with a porpoise and got nasty.

"You're going to eat Flipper?" she had asked incredulously, looking suddenly ill. Several minutes of labored explanations had ensued about how Flipper, the aquatic star of the old TV show, was a porpoise, a mammal. And how he'd never eat a porpoise. As opposed to dolphin, which was just a fish, albeit amazingly succulent. Stuart's date that evening had seemed to grudgingly accept his explanation until their meals had arrived and he'd offered her a bite to prove his point. She'd excused herself for the ladies' room, never to return.

Which actually hadn't been a loss at all. She'd been quite a bore up to that point and her filet mignon, not to mention the baked potato stuffed with sour cream and bacon bits, had been exquisite. As blind dates went, Stuart Rumpleman gave it two thumbs up.

But now as he gazed forlornly at his plate, he thought briefly about how this time he'd even sink his teeth into good old Flipper. Ranger Porter Ricks, Bud, and Sandy would have to make do in beautiful Coral Key Park without the playful marine mammal. Stuart Rumpleman's meat-starved cravings needed Flipper far more than they did. Or at least it seemed that way, because what confronted him now was a bowl of artichoke soup and a plate full of grilled tofu, lima beans, and rutabagas.

Stuart forced as broad a smile as he could muster, nodded, and said, "Looks great."

Tia beamed.

But his taste buds cried out that he was a carnivore. Those sharp incisors were made for tearing meat, not tofu. His salivary glands didn't react to a rutabaga. They reacted to a Big Mac, a Whopper, or a Wendy's bacon double cheeseburger. Or even better, one of each. This vegetarian swill just wasn't natural. After his first day with Tia, all that roughage had given him so much gas that a single match lit anywhere near him could have blown up most of Boston.

Admittedly, his digestive system had eventually adjusted. He was over the natural gas crisis. But he wasn't over the craving.

Why couldn't he deny himself and still be happy? This was, after all, the Woman of His Dreams. And meat repulsed her. He could handle one vegetarian meal, no problem. Or two or three. But they'd been together for more than a month now.

Thirty-three days. Not that he'd been counting.

He hadn't touched meat for thirty-three days. Not for breakfast, lunch, or dinner. Not for snacks. Not when he was with Tia. Not when he was away from her. Thirty-three days! And he was no mere fan of food. As his doctor had once said in exasperation, Stuart didn't eat to live. He lived to eat.

And in the last month, food had become an endless stream of eggplant and radicchio sandwiches, cabbage cakes, lentil soup, turnips, tofu, braised onion-and-mushroom stir-fry, gingered leek-and-fennel flans, Brussels sprouts, and broccoli pesto.

What was on tap for tomorrow? Eggplant upside-down spinach with a split-pea crust? It was all his fault, of course. He stabbed a lima bean with his fork and began to chew.

———

"WOULD you mind terribly if I joined you?" she had asked.

Stuart had been sitting alone at a table at T. Anthony's, a popular pizzeria on Boston's Commonwealth Avenue. A Boston University hockey game had just let out and the place was packed. He had just placed his order—a large pizza with pepperoni, sausage, and ham—when she walked in.

She was the most astonishing creature he'd ever seen.

With a model's face, high cheekbones, and perfect white teeth; a to-die-for body that a single glance confirmed was perfect in every way; and long, flowing, blonde hair.

Stuart, who looked like a middle-aged version of Flounder, the misfit in the movie *Animal House*, felt his heart slip into arrhythmia. This goddess was talking to *him*. Was asking to join *him*.

A cardiac infarction seemed imminent. His mouth became dry, his tongue like a wad of cotton. This kind of thing didn't happen to guys like him.

Nothing happened to guys like him.

"Actually, I was reserving this seat for someone really attractive," he heard himself saying to his utter disbelief. "But I guess you'll do."

She blinked. There was silence for what seemed like minutes. And then she burst out laughing.

"Humor really is the ultimate aphrodisiac, don't you think?" she asked, sitting down. "By the way, my name is Tia."

Hearing the word *aphrodisiac* pass her lips made him dizzy.

"Humor is like the nectar of the gods," he said, in an exaggerated Harvardian fashion, to his further self-amazement. Then he grinned.

Where had that come from? He'd never been able to carry on small talk before, but here he was with the most divine creature who'd ever deigned to speak with him and, while it wasn't exactly material that would get him invited on *Letterman*, his chatter was somehow amusing her. Her blue eyes sparkled. Her white teeth flashed as her laughter echoed in his ears. She was physical perfection.

And in no time, Stuart Rumpleman found that Tia was not just exquisitely beautiful, she was his soul mate. She loved John D. MacDonald's Travis McGee novels and all but the earliest William Goldman. She not only read short stories—that alone made her one in a million—but she too, considered Harlan Ellison the art form's most accomplished practitioner since Poe.

She loved *Casablanca* and all the other old Humphrey Bogart films, even though they were in (gasp!) black and white. And her "Here's looking at you kid," impersonation was delightfully almost as bad as Stuart's.

She could then gracefully slide into the time-honored debates of Ted Williams vs. Joe DiMaggio, Bill Russell vs. Wilt Chamberlain, Jim Brown vs. Gail Sayers, and she knew that Bobby Orr vs. anybody was a waste of time and breath. She adored *Bach's Brandenburg Concerto No. 2* and Charlie Parker's "Ornithology," while still remaining a fan of Aerosmith and the Black Crowes.

Stuart wondered fleetingly what this astonishing creature could possibly see in a nebbish like himself. Then he banished the thought. He would not be like Groucho Marx, refusing to join any club that would have him as a member. Perhaps opposites attracted, after all. Beauty and the Beast, right? After all, some women found Jack Nicholson attractive, didn't they?

He and Tia were tuned to the same wavelength. In the space of minutes, they had forged a link that dreams were made of. They were really, truly, honest-to-goodness, right for each other. Suddenly, she put her hand on his and a pained look came to her face.

"Please, please, tell me that you don't eat meat," she said. "I could never love someone who eats animals. Meat is just so repulsive. Dairy products, I can accept. I don't touch them myself, but I try to have an open mind. But meat..." She shuddered in disgust.

He blinked, and licked his lips. His tongue felt like cotton.

"It's immoral, too," she continued, "when you consider its effect on world hunger. It's ethically bankrupt, that's what it is. You *are* a vegetarian, aren't you?"

Stuart Rumpleman suddenly experienced a foxhole conversion. Like soldiers who made good with their Maker as they stared death in the face, Stuart looked into Tia's blue eyes and swore to himself that he would never touch meat again. Broccoli and spinach and cucumbers were his friends.

"Of course," he heard himself say. "The health benefits alone are indisputable. It's astonishing that anyone eats flesh these days. It's...it's practically barbaric!"

He wondered for a moment if this new small talk voice inside his head was laying it on too thick, but the concern proved baseless.

"I'm so relieved!" she said, and ran a finger along his palm.

Suddenly, the foxhole convert felt a chill go up and down his spine. The pizza! He couldn't very well bring his pepperoni, sausage, and ham pizza back to the table after having just espoused the virtues of a vegetarian lifestyle. They had to get out of here and fast.

"You want to go somewhere else?" he asked.

"Sure. How about my place?" she asked. "It's just two blocks from here and I'm a great cook."

———

AFTER THE FIRST totally vegetarian meal of Stuart's life, he and Tia continued their feast in the bedroom. Food had always held a near-erotic quality for him, but it had never actually been part of a sexual experience.

But on this night, Tia showed him things he'd never even imagined, and he had imagined a lot. And when he thought it couldn't get any better, she directed the *pièce de résistance*. At her behest, he placed pineapple rings on her breasts so that her nipples poked out of the circular holes. Stuart then poured lightly warmed Hershey's chocolate syrup into the empty center of the each pineapple slice, covering Tia's nipples.

He then licked the syrup off as she shuddered, and nibbled the pineapple. When she returned the favor in the strategically optimal place, Stuart knew that his cheese-burger days were over.

———

EXCEPT THEY WEREN'T.

He was in love with this goddess, no question about that. The sex wasn't just great. It was mind-boggling. It wasn't all pineapples and chocolate syrup. Sometimes it was just good old-fashioned coitus. But that was unbelievable, too.

They were eating like rabbits and screwing like rabbits. And it wasn't just sex, as if there'd be anything wrong with that. They were *making love*, experiences that were both intensely physical and at the same time powerfully emotional, bordering on the spiritual. He'd always considered that sort of thing to be the stuff of bad romance novels and sappy chick flicks. But it didn't feel that way to Stuart now. For an ugly duckling who had never been loved, his transformation into a swan, at least in Tia's eyes, filled a lonely emptiness that he'd felt in his heart for as long as he could remember. He was happier than he ever could have imagined.

Except...

Except he couldn't get his mind off what Tia considered the forbidden fruit. Every cell in his body cried out for meat. A filet mignon. A drumstick. Anything but this Brussels sprouts and turnips crap that Tia insisted on seven days a week.

It had nothing to do with that oldest of sexist phrases that some guys used after hearing about the perfect woman: "Yeah, but can she cook?" Stuart would gladly cook, just like he had all his adult life. He could marinate some steak tips or fry some sausage. He could grill anything from shrimp to swordfish. Unfortunately, however, he knew nothing about cooking with celery, cucumbers, or bean curd. Could you fry a turnip? Could you grill a rutabaga? To cook a meal in this bewildering meatless world would expose that he was a fraud.

Besides, Tia was a spectacular cook, if you liked that sort of thing. And to be honest, he could probably adjust to squash and zucchini and all their boring relatives if only there wasn't at the same time a fence around the entire animal kingdom. Adam and Eve had their forbidden Tree of the Knowledge of Good and Evil that they couldn't stay away from. Pandora had her box that she just had to open. And Stuart Rumpleman still lusted for meat.

Eventually he strayed.

He was at lunch with some of his associates at work. They had just polished off a big presentation and were out celebrating on the corporate tab. He'd raised a few eyebrows in recent weeks with his sudden affection for the plant kingdom, but today they seemed more preoccupied with their own choices and blowing off the steam built up during work on the presentation.

The menu seemed to read *meat, meat,* and then some more *meat.* As his co-workers began to order all the foods that his body craved, his salivary glands revved into warp overdrive. One time wouldn't hurt, he told himself.

Tia's voice answered in his head. *"I could never love someone who eats animals."*

But she isn't here, he thought, *and what she doesn't know won't hurt her. She isn't my mother.*

"Please, please tell me that you don't eat meat."

When we eat vegetables, Stuart told himself, they probably scream in pain, too.

"Meat is just so repulsive."

It's really none of her business, Stuart thought.

The voice of Tia in his head became silent.

"I'll have the prime rib, king size, medium rare," he said. "And I'll also have the fisherman's platter."

"There goes the budget!" muttered Carl, his boss, chuckling.

"I'll pay for it myself!" snapped Stuart, to whoops of laughter around the table.

"Don't forget the Diet Coke," added Carl with a grin.

Stuart ignored his boss.

"And bring me the shrimp cocktail while we wait," Stuart added. "I could eat a horse."

When the food arrived, he barely came up for air.

———

TIA SLAPPED him hard across the face, knocking him back against the bedroom wall. He fell to the floor. He looked up in amazed silence.

He had unlocked the door to her apartment and, at the sound of her voice, rushed to the bedroom. He had decided that he wouldn't announce his transgression. What she didn't know wouldn't hurt her. Perhaps this would even be the ideal solution: he would live like a vegetarian around Tia, but maintain a secretly carnivorous side away from her.

As he entered the bedroom, he stopped and shook his head in amazement and delight. She was dressed in Victoria's Secret regalia from the best pages of the lingerie catalog: black lace that was cut low in the right places and cut high in the right places. She wore a sinfully wicked look on her face that told him there was yet another erotic surprise in store, another pleasure boundary to cross. He kissed her lips and pressed his body against hers.

And then she belted him.

In another circumstance, the look of pure fury on her face might have appeared incongruously funny, considering her attire. But there was nothing funny about her glare and the hurt in her eyes and the sinking feeling Stuart felt in the pit of his stomach.

"You didn't!" she said.

"What are you, nuts?" he asked, conjuring some righteous indignation as he climbed to his feet.

"Don't lie to me!"

She knows. Somehow she knows. Deny it, he thought. She has no proof. Even if she can read it on your face or hear it in your voice, your only hope is to deny it.

"Lie about what?" he asked.

"Give me my key and get out."

"What have I done? What's wrong with you?"

"I want the key." She began to cry. "I thought you were happy."

"I've never been happier in my life!"

She stopped crying and glared. "Then I hope it was worth it."

"I haven't done anything!" he said, his voice sounding increasingly shrill.

"I can smell it," she said softly.

A chill went up and down Stuart's back.

"I can smell a meat-eater a mile away," she said. "You chewed your breath mints, but your entire body reeks of beef. You disgust me. Give me the key, leave and don't come back. *Ever.* You're a pig and I apologize to swine everywhere for lumping them in with you. You're beneath reproach."

Stuart swallowed hard. *How could he have thrown it all away...?*

"I want the key," she said firmly.

Suddenly, a lifetime of lima beans and turnips didn't look so confining, especially not with a dessert that included nibbling strategically placed pineapple rings and slowly licking chocolate sauce off Tia's nipples.

"It was just one slip," he pleaded, realizing that he sounded pathetic, but not knowing what else to say. "I'll never do it again."

"You'll do it again, and you know it."

Stuart Rumpleman stared at her. She was right, of course. He would do it again. It was in his bones. It was in his cells. It was in his brain. Even though she had offered him his one chance at the Holy Grail of True Love, love with someone who had no business slumming with him, he still knew that if given a second chance, he'd throw it away again. He'd last a month next time. Maybe two. Maybe three. Maybe even a year, although that seemed incomprehensible.

But he'd throw it away again.

Slowly, sadly, he fished the apartment key out of his pocket.

"Can't you forgive me? I…"

What else could he say in his defense? Even if he didn't believe it, could he say that he just needed time to change? That he simply had to adjust to being a vegetarian? That he'd been a fraud—a liar—from the first moment they'd met? That someday he might be able to become deserving of her, even though right now he represented everything that she found repugnant?

"Please?" he begged.

"I forgive your deceit," she said coolly. "But I could never be attracted to you again. You disgust me now, and that can never change. It's that simple. That's how I am. That's what I told you when we first met. So please leave."

———

Stuart Rumpleman sat alone in a booth at an all-you-can-eat buffet. He'd been through the line six times already and showed no signs of slowing down.

How did the old phrase go? It's better to have loved and lost than never to have loved at all? What a crock! He knew in the deepest levels of his soul that he could never again be truly happy. Any relationship he entered into for the rest of his life would pale by comparison. Nothing else would ever match up. And other than Tia, women hadn't exactly been flocking to him over the years.

All he'd be left with would be his guilt at having thrown away his one chance at the Holy Grail. He'd been modestly unhappy before he met Tia, but over the years he'd become comfortable with his life. He'd accepted that he was Flounder from *Animal House*, possessing neither the looks nor the personality to attract the love of anyone special.

Maybe not anyone at all.

Tia had exposed that vulnerable underbelly and then ripped the stiletto of lost love through it. *Better to have loved and lost?* Not in a million years.

And to think that it had all gone up in smoke because she'd *smelled* it. Even when trapped in the web of his own fraud, he hadn't crashed like some carnivorous Casanova in a blaze of gluttonous glory. He'd gone down like a Flounder. Exposed because he reeked of beef. Guilty by virtue of smelling bad, Your Honor. Which meant that if he left the buffet right now—which he probably should, pig that he was—and passed any orthodox vegetarians, they'd be cringing at his very smell. Didn't that just sum up his whole life in a nice, neat package?

Suddenly, Stuart dropped his fork and stopped chewing. *What the…?*

Something didn't fit. Something didn't make sense. Tia had caught him because she'd smelled the beef. That's what she'd said, and he didn't doubt it for a second.

But if that were true, then back when they first met, she'd have been able to tell even more easily that he was no vegetarian. If one meal's indiscretion could be detected, then surely she had known his true nature from her first sniff.

She'd known back then at T. Anthony's that not only was he not a vegetarian, he was the direct opposite.

Had this all been a setup?

Stuart felt sick to his stomach. Had Tia selected him for a unique brand of torture, like watching an alcoholic fight off the sweats every time he walks past a bar?

Had Tia, the Dominatrix of Diet, gotten her jollies from

having a ringside seat at his destruction? Had he been just the latest in a long line of helpless misfits whose failures fulfilled her most twisted desires?

Stuart Rumpleman shook his head and sighed. He reached for the steak sauce.

SHE'S NO SHIMMER

INTRODUCTION TO "SHE'S NO SHIMMER"

This is one of two stories in this collection that first appeared in the *Fiction River* anthology series. (The other is the final story in this collection, "One-Night Stands for Love and Glory.") *Fiction River* is a wonderful, multi-genre publication. I love appearing in its pages. Every year, I look forward to the challenge of writing six new stories to fit its announced themes.

It works much like the Story-a-Week Challenge that set my writing free. Over the course of six weeks, a topic is announced on Monday, and the story is due on Sunday by midnight Pacific Time. There have been times I've been glad I live on the East Coast, giving me what feels like three extra hours. I submitted my award-winning "Death in the Serengeti" story on Monday at 2:57 a.m., three minutes before the deadline. The story was a pulse-pounding thriller; so was the submittal process.

There was no such deadline drama with "She's No Shimmer," however. The topic of ghosts was announced, and in no time my two main characters were having a conversation in a suddenly chilly Key West cabaret dressing room. I'd visited such cabarets (though no dressing rooms) during vacations at my brother, Steve's, place in Key West. I'd been astounded at the creativity of the performers and laughed uproariously at the humor.

This story fell into place quite quickly, and the editor of *Fiction River: Ghosts*, Kerrie Hughes, loved it. Sometimes an editor will buy a story but require potentially significant changes. In this case, however, only the most minor copy-editing tweaks were needed.

If only all stories moved so easily from conception to print.

Thanks to my brother, Steve, for his hospitality in Key West and for introducing me to the cabaret scene on that first New Year's Eve. Thanks also to my nephew, Jonny, for making sure I got the details right.

SHE'S NO SHIMMER

Shimmer saw that it was time. She materialized, perched atop the dark wooden dresser in the corner of her old dressing room, the slit in her sequined gown showing off her lovely legs.

She still had it.

The latest pretender hoping to fill her shoes, Chantel La Foxe, gave a start.

"You could give me some warning, you know," she said, shaking her pretty little head, ever the drama queen. "You scare the crap out of me every time."

Chantel, wearing only her breastplate and black body girdle, shivered. Retrieving a black bathrobe from the full-length closet on the right wall, she slipped into it and cinched the belt, then shivered again. The temperature in the small, windowless dressing room had plummeted, as it always did when Shimmer appeared, by fifteen degrees. The smell of strawberries filled the air.

Chantel lit a Virginia Slim menthol light and took a deep drag. She tilted her head up and exhaled a cloud of blue smoke, obscuring the three framed posters hanging on the wall above the vanity. Depicting Shimmer in her most famous roles, they served as a reminder to Chantel, as they had been to her predecessors, of the greatness to which they might aspire.

And forever fall short.

Chantel took another puff, and set the cigarette down in a glass ashtray.

"Those things will kill you," Shimmer said. She pursed her lips, knowing the whore-red lipstick stood out even more against the pallor of her cheeks.

Chantel started to say something, then stopped. She picked up the cigarette and drew in another deep drag.

"Go ahead, say it, I won't bite," Shimmer said.

Chantel exhaled again, then shrugged. "It's just an odd thing for a...for a ghost to say."

"That isn't what you were going to say. You know it, and I know it."

Chantel stared into the mirror and began applying pancake to her cheeks.

"When I said that cigarettes will kill you," Shimmer continued, "you wanted to say, 'And so will unprotected sex.'"

Chantel flushed.

"You can't hide things from me, Chantel. Don't even try."

Chantel silently applied her gaudiest fake eyelashes.

"He lied to me," Shimmer said. "We were supposed to be exclusive. He cheated on me."

And as a result, Key West's most famous female impersonator had become a name etched into the black stones of the AIDS memorial down by the White Street Pier.

Anthony "Shimmer" Rosati.

Perhaps the memorial would outlast the memories of those who'd seen her perform, but perhaps not.

Female impersonators were a dime a dozen in Key West, like wanna-be actors and actresses in Hollywood, and country music singers in Nashville. Key West was, after all, where CNN went on New Year's Eve to televise the dropping of a drag queen in a gaudy ten-foot red shoe at midnight.

But there were the average, garden-variety female impersonators and drag queens, lip-synching to everything from "It's Raining Men" to "Born This Way."

And then there were the stars.

Performers who would no more lip-synch than date a woman. Performers who brought alive the likes of Lucille Ball, Marilyn Monroe, and Carol Channing.

And in Key West, that meant only a handful of stars.

All of whom had circled the brightest one of them all: Shimmer.

Until...

Well...

Her final curtain closing was a tragic occurrence mirrored all across the globe. Shimmer received no special mercy.

Except that she now haunted the cabaret she'd made famous to the point of it being posthumously renamed in her honor, Café Rosati.

"You need to over enunciate *even more* when you're doing Lucille Ball and Carol Channing," Shimmer said. "In your last act, you were drifting toward them both sounding far too normal. The exaggeration is what makes it work."

Chantel opened her pretty mouth to speak, but said nothing.

"You know I'm right," Shimmer said.

Chantel glanced over, but averted her eyes. "I can't do Lucille Ball and Carol Channing as well as you did."

"Of course not."

"I need to do something different," Chantel said. "Change the act."

"We change the act all the time. Toss in a few new jokes. Switch up the subjects. It keeps the locals coming back for repeat performances when they have guests in town. Hell, we even dropped Cher from your repertoire—"

"But—"

"—when you added a few pounds." Shimmer knew it was a cheap shot, but she'd been unable to stop herself. Chantel had gained a couple pounds and, more importantly, as she strained the confines of her body girdle, she'd also strained the confines of her script.

Megastars could freelance. Shimmer had done it all the time, delighting audiences with her improvisational interactions.

But Chantel was no megastar. No star at all. And she never would be.

"I can't be you," Chantel said. "I hear people talk. They say, 'She's good, but she's no Shimmer.' They say it all the time."

Shimmer smiled.

"If I keep trying to be you," Chantel said, "I'll always be second-rate."

"Honey," Shimmer said. "You're always going to be second-rate, no matter what. It's either second-rate or a complete embarrassment. You'll never be a star. But you can be...serviceable.

"Stick to the script I give you or bomb out. You've got a legend guiding you. How many female impersonators would *love* to be in your shoes? They'd give their right testicle for the chance. Their left one, too. Ignore me, and people will talk about the fool who got the opportunity of a lifetime and flamed out. You'll be legendary, but only in the most humiliating way."

Chantel licked her lips, still pale and devoid of lipstick. She took a last deep drag on her cigarette, then stubbed it out fiercely. "Thanks for your honesty."

"Tough love, honey. But it's for your own good. They didn't name this place after me for nothing."

"I know I'm just a minor league talent in your eyes. I know I'll never be a legend like you. But I've got to...I'm still going to..."

Shimmer watched Chantel swallow hard. Her hands shook as she fumbled for another cigarette.

Chantel turned toward Shimmer. "Tonight, I'm doing Barbara Bush."

———

BARBARA BLEEPING BUSH.

Holy Mother of God, Shimmer thought, what was Chantel thinking? Key West was somewhere to the left of nearby Fidel Castro, so taking potshots at Republicans hardly qualified as a risk.

But doing a female impersonation of Barbara Bleeping Bush? There was...nothing to work with. The woman didn't sing, or dance, or act, or make people laugh, or...

Or anything.

There was only one Barbara in female impersonation and that was, of course, Barbra Streisand.

Barbara Bush? It boggled the mind. If Chantel insisted, she would bomb. And not just bomb a little. Bomb spectacularly.

Go up in a roaring ball of flames.

So Shimmer tried reasoning with Chantel, using all her vast insecurities against her, like a sliver under a fingernail.

But now, as the show unfolded, Shimmer suspected Chantel might just do it anyway. She'd probably chicken out...or come to her senses. Both would give the same result.

But Chantel might actually defy Shimmer.

Shimmer watched with a sense of impending horror as Chantel began with the standard warm-up. She came out as Barbra Streisand, singing, "The Way We Were," punctuating passages of legitimate cabaret singing with exaggerated lip puckering and widening and pretentious enunciations that got the crowd laughing and clapping its approval.

"Good to see all of you," Chantel said to the capacity crowd of a hundred fifty, all arrayed at circular tables seating four each with all chairs turned to see the stage. A spotlight shone down from an improvised balcony halfway back on the right.

Chantel placed a hand over her eyes and peered out at the audience. "How many homosexuals do we have out there tonight?"

Loud, enthusiastic clapping erupted.

"My people!" Chantel said.

Shimmer nodded her approval. Chantel was sticking to the script.

"How about heterosexuals?" Chantel asked. "How many out there tonight?"

Again there was loud clapping, signifying the typical 50-50 split, but the straights weren't quite as enthusiastic.

"I'm sorry," Chantel said, looking mournful. "But it's not your fault. You were born that way."

The room erupted in laughter, as it always did. It was a joke used by performers up and down Duvall Street, stolen so long ago from its original author that no one quite knew who deserved the credit. But it delighted even those who were hearing it for the tenth time.

Chantel moved off stage to change into her next costume, but continued to talk to the audience, cracking jokes about places like Peoria and Cleveland.

Sticking to the script.

Shimmer wondered why she felt so nervous. So what if Chantel went freelance and flamed out? Her equally mediocre successor would arrive, and prove no more of a threat to Shimmer's legend than her predecessors.

They'd say of the next one, just like they'd said of all of them, "She's good, but she's no Shimmer."

And Shimmer would smile her pallid, bright-red smile and feel the contentment befitting a legend.

Chantel emerged from the side of the stage, dressed as Madonna in her iconic pink cone brassiere, belted corset, and garter belts. She sang, of course, "Like A Virgin" as she stepped down from the stage and walked along the stage-right aisle, pointing to conspicuous audience members when she got to the word "virgin." While still singing, she curled the few remaining strands of hair in a balding man's pate, then took his glasses off and, while taking a breath before the next line in the song, planted her lipstick on the lens.

The audience loved it, as they always did. It was a B+ or even an A- performance. Not the stuff of legends, but serviceable.

Chantel was back up on stage by the end of the song and curtsied to the loud applause. It was pretty hard for a female impersonator to screw up that number. She ducked off-stage, then came back as Dolly Parton, with balloons for boobs.

Chantel continued perfectly on script. She referred to

her new measurements as forty-four, twenty-eight, thirty-eight, nine and a half.

The crowd roared.

It was all part of the script, the jokes copied by other performers far and wide. Chantel even spotted an opportunity for an approved "improvisation," every bit as scripted as the rest of the show, but possible only when the right audience members were in the right position.

"Are the two of you a couple?" Chantel asked as the spotlight illuminated a photogenic young man and woman in their early twenties, sitting in the front row of tables.

They both nodded enthusiastically.

Chantel got their names, Jason and Cindy, and focused on the young woman. "Is he good in bed?"

As everyone else laughed, so did Cindy, covering her mouth with one hand and nodding.

Chantel shook her head in mock disappointment. "That's not a very enthusiastic response. Tell the truth. Tell little old Chantel La Foxe. I won't tell a soul. He's a dud, isn't he?"

The young woman shook her head, but like the rest of the audience, was laughing so hard she could barely speak. She finally managed, "He's great!"

"Really?"

"Yes!"

Chantel turned to the young man, and sounding like a man for the first time in the show, said in a low, masculine voice, "You go both ways?"

The room erupted. Shimmer began to relax. All of Chantel's talk about trying something new had been just that. Talk. She'd smartened up and realized that second-rate talents don't question the legends. They don't make waves. They follow directions and put the lyric widget in position

A, the melodic gizmo in position B, and the comic widget in position C.

They kept the assembly line moving.

And with each performance, or at worse every few performances, the phrase "She's no Shimmer" would be uttered one or two more times, a phrase that never grew old.

"Are you married?" Chantel asked the couple.

They both shook their heads.

Chantel looked at the woman with dismay. "You're giving it away for free?"

More scripted improvisation. More laughter.

"We're engaged," the woman said.

"You're engaged," Chantel said in apparent delight. "Can I see the ring?"

The woman thrust the ring forward and Chantel bent to look at it, fumbling a bit with her Dolly Parton boobs, but quickly returning attention to this woman, Cindy. "It's beautiful," Chantel said. "That's quite a diamond, but...it'd be bigger if you swallowed."

Again, the room erupted, and with the scripted improvisation at its end, Chantel launched into Dolly Parton singing a song about mountains, and on each line she knocked one of her giant boobs out of alignment to the amusement of all.

It was a show that had been performed a thousand times.

Until...

Chantel curtsied, shifted Dolly's boobs finally into alignment, then ducked off stage to make her next costume change.

"This is where I'd usually switch into the Liza Minnelli character," Chantel said, "but I suspect lots of you have seen more than enough of Liza. You'd like something completely new, completely different. Would you like that?"

The audience roared its approval. They'd been primed to give an enthusiastic response to anything.

Shimmer was beside Chantel in a flash, knowing she couldn't allow this to go forward. It was time to play her trump card. "What do you think you're doing? Go ahead with this stunt and you'll never work in this town again. I guarantee it.

"Never. Work. Again."

None of Shimmer's words came over the room's sound system. Either the sound engineer, Chantel's husband, had cut the feed, or Shimmer's words had been translated to the sound of rushing wind that filled the room.

But the words came out loud and clear for Chantel. Shimmer could see it in her frightened face and wide eyes. A sliver of resolve remained, until Shimmer mentioned the names of three of Chantel's predecessors who had challenged Shimmer and lost. She'd seen to their professional demise.

"All three of them thought they knew better than I did," Shimmer said. "They were laughed out of town, and I don't mean laughter in a good way. They...never...worked...again."

Chantel's quivering voice cut through the noise of rushing wind. "Change of plans."

The crowd groaned.

She poked her head around the curtain. "I was going to play Barbara Bush, but..." She smiled. "To do that, I've got to gain another fifty pounds."

The audience chuckled. Some even laughed, though it wasn't the uproarious mirth of seconds before. Most likely, the line would have fallen flat had the crowd not spent the last half-hour laughing its collective asses off. There were a few too many members with matronly figures like the former First Lady who weren't prepared to mock themselves about such a sensitive topic.

But it didn't stop the show's momentum dead in its tracks. In short order, Chantel emerged, skipping Liza, as she'd planned all along, but returning to script with Marilyn Monroe.

Crisis averted.

———

"I SHOULD HAVE KEPT GOING," Chantel said in the dressing room after the show. "I can't believe I let you change my mind."

"You saved your career by listening to me," Shimmer said.

"I can't live with myself if I don't try," Chantel said. "Next time, I'm going to do it. You can't stop me. Not unless you smother me in my sleep."

"It's a thought," Shimmer said.

Chantel glared. This time there were no averted eyes. She flung the black Tina Turner wig onto the vanity. "I'm not going to keep doing a pale imitation of you forever. It's even more pale—" She nodded at Shimmer. "—than you are. Smother me in my sleep if you want, but if you don't, you'll have to wrestle me down next time to stop me."

Shimmer glared back at the impertinence. The ingratitude. The arrogance.

"And with all that extra weight you're always nagging me about," Chantel said, "I'm sure I can whip your ass."

———

AT THE NEXT PERFORMANCE, two nights later, Chantel moved smoothly through the script, just like before. She even found a perfect engaged couple, this time Jennifer and Ryan, to banter with and repeated the previous night's "improvisation."

Then Chantel got to the point of departure.

Shimmer watched, grim-faced and sure her student was about to humiliate herself, as Chantel prepped the crowd.

"This is where I'd usually switch into the Liza Minnelli character," she said, as she had two nights earlier, "but I suspect lots of you have seen more than enough of Liza. You'd like something completely new, completely different. Would you like that?"

As had been the case before, the audience roared its approval.

"I present to you," Chantel said, "Barbara Bush."

She walked on stage, white-haired and looking matronly, wrapped in enough padding around her body girdle to look like she'd gained eighty pounds, but all of it covered by a suitably frumpy dress. She looked very much like the former First Lady.

The audience broke into nervous laughter. A few people gasped.

"I believe this is the first female impersonation of Barbara Bush. Ever. And the first time for everything can be a little awkward. Even painful," Chantel said.

"Ladies, let's think back to our first time. A little uncomfortable, am I right?" Chantel turned to Jennifer, the woman who'd been part of this evening's scripted improvisation, a cute redhead with a sparkling smile. "Isn't that right, Jennifer?"

Jennifer nodded.

"But it got better, right, Jennifer? Now you enjoy it, right?"

Jennifer nodded and smiled.

"And what about the first time up the ass?"

The room erupted.

"Right, Jennifer? It gets better, right?"

Jennifer laughed, turning bright red, but covered her face and shook her head no.

"No?" Chantel turned to the boyfriend. Switching to her low, masculine voice, Chantel said, "Don't worry, Ryan, I'll show you how."

The gays in the crowd howled and the straights followed along, albeit nervously.

Shimmer felt herself shiver as Chantel's gambles kept paying off. A former First Lady talking about anal sex? And there hadn't even been a song. At least, not yet. God knew what it might be.

Like a high wire act without a net, Chantel was stepping out onto the wire, fearless. Reckless. Brainless, in fact. The chances she was taking were insane.

And then the memories came back to Shimmer. Long, long ago. Some of the insane chances she had taken in the early days, some of which had paid off, and others not. And when they hadn't, well, she'd dusted herself off and tried again. And when they had paid off, those had become part of her legend.

Suddenly, Shimmer felt cold. So very, very cold. Almost freezing. She wrapped her arms around herself, but saw that the pallor of her skin had gone from pale to almost transparent.

She shivered uncontrollably.

Back on stage, Chantel continued. "I'm Barbara Bush," she said in a voice that seemed very, very distant. "I can't sing or dance, and I'm not beautiful. But I sure know how to perform.

"Being married to Georgie for all these years made it a requirement. He might have been the Commander in Chief, but he wasn't equipped with a howitzer."

A cold wind whipped around Shimmer.

So very, very cold. Her hands shook. Her teeth chattered.

As Chantel's voice faded into near imperceptibility, Shimmer thought, *That little bitch is pulling it off! Barbara Bleeping Bush. It's brilliant!*

Shimmer could barely make out the laughter. Shocked laughter, like she'd heard so very long ago.

Chantel squeaked in an old woman's voice. "Is it in yet?"

Distant, distant laughter.

"Oh, Georgie. Give it to me, Georgie..."

The laughter erupted, but was racing away from Shimmer.

Farther and farther away.

Shimmer felt impossibly cold.

And then, her light, which had blazed so brilliantly and for so very long, flickered...

...and flickered...

...and with a soft, satisfied pop, went out.

BELOVED

INTRODUCTION TO "BELOVED"

Trust me, you would not have wanted to read my first attempt at this story.

At the time, I hadn't even heard what Kris and Dean would soon teach me about the creative and analytical sides of the brain. The fateful Master Class was still a half year in the future. I was still "a slow writer," unknowingly trying to create with the analytical side of my brain firmly applying not only the brakes but the emergency brakes, too.

I couldn't get out of my own way.

I had signed up for what was then called the Denise Little Anthology Workshop. Denise was editing two anthologies for DAW, and those of us attending the workshop would have the opportunity to submit for them. The prospect of actually appearing in an anthology—in a real book!—made my heart pound.

We had a few weeks before the workshop to write a story for *Swordplay,* an anthology about swords. The story for the other anthology, however, would be written at the workshop. I made my best attempt at a *Swordplay* story, then waited for the workshop, knowing in my heart of hearts that I'd produce only a colossal failure with the second story.

I hadn't been at the Story-a-Week challenge for that long, and writing a story in one week felt like a breakneck pace. The prospect of writing one in barely more than twenty-four hours seemed impossible.

The theme for *The Trouble With Heroes* was announced on the first workshop night. Though it was referred to as an "overnight" story, I believe two nights were involved before the morning deadline, but the day between included classes. I needed at least a week to write a story. How could I possibly write one in barely more than a day, especially when I would still be attending classes?

The topic intrigued me, but the deadline filled my heart with panic. So did "the competition," the other writers who would also be submitting stories. Writers aren't really in competition with each other, but I was intimidated by the list of credits some of them could claim—multiple published novels!—while almost all I'd known in the fiction world was failure.

There was no way I could write a story with such a deadline. And if I did manage *something*, there was no way it could compare favorably to what such accomplished writers would produce.

I had no chance at all.

But I was going to give it my best shot. Figuring all the good writers, namely everyone but me, would take classic heroes for their stories, I went off the beaten path. That's actually a perfect strategy when writing for anthologies because if there are two terrific but similar stories, often only one of them can be selected. An editor wants variety.

I didn't know all of that. I just knew fear and intimidation. I lucked into a successful strategy. So as a preacher's kid with better knowledge of Biblical heroes than those of Greek and Roman mythology that I figured would be the popular choices, I headed for the Old Testament and King David.

The story was a train wreck. Predictably. After all, I was still creating with the brakes and emergency brakes on. I completed it, thanks to a near all-nighter, and submitted it on time, but I wanted to wear a bag over my head.

It was *awful*. Beyond embarrassing. It was downright humiliating.

Its only saving grace was its opening line.

There's nothing like a man holding the severed head of a giant to get a woman in the mood.

If you don't think that's a killer opening line, then I give up. There's no convincing you. I loved that opening. But everything that followed was wretched beyond belief.

Denise Little was gentle in her comments. She said the story didn't work at all, but that opening line was a winner. It was the best from all the stories submitted. I should take that opening line, throw out all the rest and try something totally different. If I could send her the new story within a week, she'd look at it.

I went home and tried again. Once I figured out the correct point-of-view character, the story fell into place.

Denise bought it.

And when a year or so later *The Trouble With Heroes* appeared on the local bookstore's shelves, I couldn't buy enough copies.

BELOVED

There's nothing like a man holding the severed head of a giant to get a woman in the mood.

It did nothing for me, but my younger sister, Michal, looked to be in heat. Her pretty little face flushed. Her bosom, more ample than mine, heaved. Her breath came in short, quick gasps.

"He's *so* handsome," she said.

Atop a platform that overlooked the palace courtyard, David lifted Goliath's head and shook it. The crowd roared. Women danced and beat upon their tambourines. Men still decked out in their battlefield attire raised their spears and shouted. Clouds of dust rose up to us on the royal balcony beside the platform.

"Look at those eyes," Michal gushed.

She was becoming insufferable. "What if the stone missed the giant?" I asked. "Would he still be so handsome? What if he ran from the fight, so terrified he soiled his loincloth? Would his eyes still be so pretty?"

A pout formed on Michal's lips. "You're such a cynic, Merab. There's not a man in Israel that could impress you."

She finally tore her eyes away from David. "If Father expects to marry you away first, I might die a virgin."

Father would have no trouble marrying me off; he was the king. But Michal would be the prize. She was the pretty one. I was plain. Serviceable. Like a healthy donkey.

"Maybe I don't want marry," I said.

She shook her head in that way that said she'd never understand me. "Well, I do." Her cheeks burned red. "David, son of Jesse," she said. "I'm going to marry him some day."

I raised my eyebrows. "Does he know?"

"You can be so—"

She gasped and touched my arm. "He's coming this way!"

David strode to our side of the platform, his eyes fixed on Michal. Following behind him were my father, King Saul, and my brother, Jonathan. I'd heard David had been a humble shepherd, but those days were no more. He looked drunk with the glory being showered upon him.

Michal gripped my arm tighter. I thought she might fall over into a dead faint.

David bent one knee and bowed his head. "King Saul's daughters are as fair as this day is great."

A smooth talker. As if Michal weren't already smitten.

"Tell us of your feat, O Champion," she said.

David beamed. "The Lord God Jehovah slew the giant. I was but his instrument."

Clever, I thought. The obligatory deference followed by a proud retelling.

Her voice quivering, Michal asked, "Will you deny the king's daughter your story?"

"Of course not." David smiled. "The giant threatened all of Israel, commanding us to send one man who would fight him. Your father, the King, offered me his armor, helmet, and coat of mail, but I took them off. Instead, I chose five smooth stones from a brook and put one within my sling. The first one struck the giant in the head and he toppled to the ground. I fell upon him and, using his own sword, cut off his head."

David shook the giant's head again, setting off another roar from the crowd.

"This was your first time in battle?" Michal asked.

David flushed.

My sweet, pretty sister had not the sense of the flies buzzing about the giant's head.

"Yes," David said, "but while tending my father's sheep, I defended the flock by killing a lion and a bear with my own hands."

"*A lion?*" Michal gasped. "And a bear? With your own hands?"

So much, I thought, for deference to the Lord God Jehovah.

"I caught the creature by its beard, struck it, and killed it."

"Such bravery!" Michal said.

I stifled a laugh. *If* there had been a lion or bear, I was pretty sure that what had protected the flock was a rock within David's sling. There'd been no wrestling the beast to the ground, much less beating it to death with David's bare hands. It was a nice tale to charm the young women of the kingdom, but I didn't believe it.

The way his chest swelled with pride, though, I suspected he'd come to believe the tale himself. Vanity at its worst.

"Your mother, the Queen, awaits our appearance inside the palace," David said. He looked at Michal. "Perhaps we shall meet again."

"Yes," she said, looking as though she might throw herself off the balcony to him.

David bowed and turned away.

———

FOR THE NEXT FEW DAYS, every time I spotted Michal with that love-struck look in her eyes, I said, "He's beating another lion to death right now. With his bare hands!" I'd gasp and add, "Such bravery!"

She'd glare or perhaps throw something at me as I burst into laughter, but eventually she began to laugh too.

"He was trying to impress me, that's all," she said. "There's no harm in a little embellishment. He can't be *perfect*."

"Of course," I said. "Just trying to impress. I'm sure he's as smitten with you as you are with him." Then I mimicked her dreamy-eyed look.

"That's not funny, Merab," she said.

"You should see yourself."

A pout came over her lips. "Will you speak to Father about David for me? He listens to you. He treats me as if I'm still a child."

I gave her the look. "I wonder why."

"I'm a woman now," she said defensively. "Just because you're the eldest doesn't make me any less a woman."

She waited. "Will you?"

I didn't respond right away. I thought the one person David was most smitten by was himself. Drunk with the chants of the crowd.

Or was I just being jealous, upset that the good-looking hero favored Michal with his attention while ignoring me?

"Don't help me," she finally said, bitterness in her voice. "Forget I asked. You're as evil as you pretend to be."

"Oh, stop," I said and agreed to help her.

———

I GOT my chance sooner than I expected.

Father summoned me to his side in one of his chambers. We sat at a table and Father dismissed his guards, telling them to wait outside. He drank deeply from a cup and sighed. Mother sat beside him, looking pleased.

He got right to the point. "It is time that you be wed," he said. "You have become a woman and it is right that, as God provided Adam and Eve for each other, you should have a mate."

If Michal had made reference to Adam and Even during one of her endless discussions about true love, I'd have asked how well that one had worked out. But that didn't seem to be the right thing to say now.

I wanted to beg for more time. A year. Two years. Ten years. A lifetime. I wasn't ready for a man. I doubted that I'd ever be ready.

But I said, "Yes, Father."

He nodded. "Adriel, the son of Barzillai the Meholathite, has offered a dowry fitting for a king's daughter."

Father ran through a list of all of the man's virtues, chiefly being that he was rich enough to afford my dowry, but I barely listened.

Why couldn't I be like Michal, enthused about marriage? Most girls were like her. Or at least they were more accepting of the prospect than I was.

I cringed at the thought of a foul-smelling brute climbing atop me and inserting something repulsive into my most private place, all so I could get a baby inside me. A baby that would then hurt so much coming out that, by comparison, I wouldn't think the act that got it there in the first place was so awful.

Maybe I talked to the servant girls too much. Or to the wrong ones. Still, I didn't understand why anyone would look forward to that.

But I knew my place, so when Father finished, I said, "It would please me greatly to marry the man you have chosen. I hope that God will bless me with many male children."

Father and Mother nodded and smiled.

I felt like running from the room, but remembered my promise so I asked, "When will Michal marry? She, too, is a woman now."

They both were taken aback.

"After your marriage," Father said. "You are the eldest. Why do you ask?"

"Have you considered joining our house to David, son of Jesse?"

Father's face clouded over. He gripped the sides of his chair so tightly, his hands shook. "Must I hear his name from you too? Will even my own household speak of him?"

His eyes blazed and he began to shout. "Have you heard the chants when we return from battle? 'Saul has killed his thousands. David has killed his ten thousands.' What else is left for him? To take away my kingdom?"

I bowed my head, hoping that the madness would not overtake him. "Father, I meant no harm. Forgive my tongue for I speak when I should be quiet." I took a chance. "Though not as often as Michal."

He glared at me for a time, his face red, but then burst into laughter. "Not as often as Michal." He roared. "Of that you are right. That girl is never quiet."

I took one more chance. "Father, you are the king, the first one given by God to Israel. You need fear no poor shepherd's son. But if David's popularity becomes a danger, marry him to one of your daughters. Then he becomes an ally."

Father stared in wonderment. Mother looked on with confused fear, her gaze moving back between Father and me.

"He is but the youngest son of a poor shepherd," Father said. "How could he pay a dowry fitting a king's daughter?"

I drew in a deep breath. "Is not an ally worth more than any dowry a richer man could pay?"

Silence filled the room for a long time.

Then Father nodded, a smile forming upon his lips. "You have wisdom greater than all my advisors." He glanced at Mother and said, "So it shall be."

MICHAL SHRIEKED with delight and hugged me, begging forgiveness for all the times she'd called me evil. Over and over, she pried me for details I might have forgotten.

Days later, we were summoned before the throne. We wore jewels and our finest tunics, covering our heads even though that wasn't required until the actual wedding ceremony.

As the eldest, I went first while Michal remained in a rear antechamber. Mother and I stood behind Father's throne as the guards stepped outside. Flowers adored the walls. A musician played the lute and sang. I awaited Adriel the Meholathite.

In walked David.

I froze. What was he doing here? I glanced at Mother. She beamed.

When the lute player finished, Father began. "David, son of Jesse, you have become the greatest warrior in the kingdom," he said. "I have summoned you today to repay you. I offer my daughter's hand in marriage. Merab will make you a good wife and bear you many male children. I require only that you be valiant for me and fight the Lord's battles."

David's ruddy complexion turned pale. He looked to me. I averted my eyes. Michal would be furious. David didn't look too happy about it either.

"Oh, great king," he finally said. "Who am I? I am the least of all men, the youngest son of a poor shepherd from the least of the tribes. Who am I to be a son-in-law to the king?"

Heavy silence fell over the court.

He had rejected me? I wanted none of this man. I wanted none of any man. But to be offered to *a poor shepherd* and then scorned made me want to cover my head in shame. I had never felt such humiliation. I might not be pleasing to the eye, but I was the king's daughter.

"But...the people love you," Father said. "You are not the least of all men." Appearing unable to comprehend David's rejection, Father said, "I require no dowry but that you serve me in battle."

David bowed his head. "It is a great and kind offer, O King, but I cannot accept. Please offer Merab's hand to a man more worthy than I."

More worthy? His vanity knew no bounds, his chest swelling with pride when the people chanted of the king killing his thousands and David his ten thousands. He claimed not to be worthy?

I knew who he considered unworthy. Me!

Not that I wanted him, but had ever there been a king's daughter offered with no dowry but loyalty? That would be shame enough. But for such a woman to be considered so repugnant that even such an offer was refused was beyond the pale.

I ran from all these witnesses to my shame, and burst into the antechamber where Michal waited, almost knocking her over.

Mother followed behind. Her face ashen, she said, "Michal, go to your father. He awaits you."

Startled and confused, she left.

I buried my face in my hands. This was the problem with heroes. They became so filled with pride that even the lowliest of them—a poor shepherd!—could reject the hand of a king's daughter.

———

MICHAL FLEW BACK into the room in a cold rage. "You said you talked to Father!"

"I did, but he—"

"You stole David away from me! You don't love him. You only speak of him with scorn. How could you have done this?"

"I spoke for you, Michal, but Father heard what he wanted to hear."

"But—"

"Michal!" I said. "David rejected me."

She blinked. "*Neither* of us is getting married?"

I nodded.

"Because of the dowry?"

In a voice barely above a whisper, I said, "There was no dowry. David had to only pledge his loyalty."

Michal's eyes widened and for a time she said no more. Finally, she asked, "Do you think...he loves me?"

———

So I married Adriel the Meholathite.

Marriage hasn't been as bad as I imagined. Only on the six days leading up to the Sabbath do I pray that the Lord God strike me dead.

Father offered Michal's hand to David, though this time with a dowry to be earned on the battlefield. With me out of the way, David no longer felt unworthy of being the king's son-in-law.

What a surprise.

I still believe that David's vanity will one day cause Michal pain as it does for so many who love heroes, but I've come to believe that he loves her too.

Perhaps it is one of those lies we tell ourselves often enough until we believe it—like David's killing of the lion and bear with his own hands—but I now accept that David's refusal was not a rejection of me but rather that he loved Michal and could accept no other.

That I can forgive.

For I cannot question his devotion.

You know a man is in love when he pays a dowry of two hundred Philistine foreskins.

GOING DRY

INTRODUCTION TO "GOING DRY"

For a long time at US College Hockey Online, I covered Hockey East all by myself. Oh, we added arena reporters who wrote game stories for each team. But I wrote all the columns, almost all the features, and had my pick of the games to cover each weekend.

Hockey East was my beat, and I was proud of my work.

But as I described in this book's introduction, fiction had to become a priority. And so, at first grudgingly, I turned the column and choice weekend games over to another writer every third or fourth week. It gave me extra time for what I really loved most.

Over time, that "other writer" became my good friend, Jim Connelly. And what had been every third or fourth week became every third, and then every other week. Then the balance of responsibilities shifted even more. Now, Jim writes the columns two out of every three weeks, if not three out of every four.

Fiction is my first love, not college hockey or writing about it.

Priorities.

Jim and I have shared not just the Hockey East beat, but many laughs. One of them is how as a student, he was the equipment manager for his school's team. The team had advanced to the Hockey East semifinals, held the day after St. Patrick's Day. The coach read the team the riot act that there was to be no St. Patrick's Day drinking.

None. Not even by the Irish players.

Not even by the Irish equipment manager.

Jim, who has been known to have a Jack-and-Coke or six, had to go totally dry on a day meant for Irish celebration.

That story of his led to this one of mine. It's short, but sweet.

Thanks, Jim.

GOING DRY

Devin Patrick O'Donnell had been leaning against the splintered door frame but stood up straight, hairs prickling on the back of his neck. "You're what?"

Megan's smile faltered and her lower lip quivered ever so slightly. "I'm pregnant."

The next words slipped out before he realized it. "How'd that happen?"

Megan, a petite redhead who was the prettiest girl in Southie as far as Devin was concerned, flinched.

"I didn't mean it that way," Devin said. "What I meant—"

"I know what you meant, Devin Patrick."

The door to her parent's second-floor apartment slammed, leaving him alone on the musty, dimly lit landing. Creaky wooden stairs curled up to the third floor and descended to the ground.

Devin knocked on the door. "Megan, open up."

"Go away!"

"Let me explain."

"Go away!"

Devin felt a tap on his knee.

"In some trouble, me lad?" The leprechaun sported a wide-brimmed hat, a brass-buckled belt, and clothes of emerald green. He stood less than thigh-high to Devin and smelled faintly of corned beef and cabbage. "May I be of service to ye?"

Devin Patrick O'Donnell gaped.

The leprechaun bowed. "Cat got ye tongue?"

"Who're you?"

"Not very friendly, are you there? Not to someone who can solve all your problems."

Devin looked at him askance. "What do you think you can do for me?"

"Pot 'o gold, laddie." The dandy smiled. "I can point you to a pot 'o gold."

"What would that solve?"

"Why, buy her a diamond ring, of course. Make her an honest woman," the leprechaun said.

"How'd you know about that?"

The leprechaun smiled. "Laddie, I know about a lot of t'ings."

Devin cocked his head. "What do I have to do, sell you my soul?"

The little green man looked indignant. He tucked his thumbs inside his belt. "Ye owe me an apology. I'm not the devil."

"What are you? Who are you?"

"The name be Thomas. And if ye don't know what I am, then ye best be on your way."

Devin eyed the leprechaun warily. "So this pot of gold..." he said. "Not that I believe it, but...what do you expect me to do?"

"Aye, that's more like it, me boy." Thomas patted Devin on the back of his knee. "What day be tomorrow?"

"Thursday."

"No, what *day* be it?"

Devin blinked. "Oh. St. Paddy's Day."

"Right ye are, me boy. Right ye are. And a strange St. Paddy's Day it will be for you." The leprechaun clapped Devin's knee. "To earn that pot 'o gold, all ye must do is one thing. Ye must spend the day with me, from morning till midnight, and not touch a drop of the spirits."

———

DEVIN HAD HEARD ABOUT LEPRECHAUNS. How they were mischievous. Schemers. You had to keep an eye on them at all times.

But St. Paddy's Day without a beer? The last time he'd spent St. Patrick's Day sober, he'd been thirteen. Nine years ago.

Devin bellied up to the bar, slid onto a stool and feeling painfully conspicuous, lifted Thomas onto another.

Clancy, the white-haired bartender, stopped polishing the mug in his hand. "That be one hell of a costume, little man."

"Thank ye, kind sir." Still standing on the stool, Thomas tipped the brim of his emerald hat. "I'll have me a Guinness."

Devin averted his eyes. "Diet Coke."

Clancy looked as if someone had just taken a dump on his corned beef and cabbage. "Say that again, lad."

"Diet Coke."

"Ah, bejesus," Clancy said, shaking his head. "What's this world coming to?"

The leprechaun winked. "I'm enjoying meself already." When his Guinness arrived, he slurped it down, slammed the mug down onto the bar, and smacked his lips. "Another one, kind sir, to wet me whistle!"

Devin wasn't sure this was worth all the pots of gold in the world combined. Everyone's eyes were on the two spectacles: Thomas pounding down his Guinness and Devin trying to hide his Diet Coke.

"What a fine St. Paddy's Day this be." Thomas clapped Devin on the shoulder. "Ye ready for another Diet Coke, laddie?" He laughed. "This be worth the price of admission."

Soon other patrons surrounded the two. While looking askance at their native son suddenly turned effete, they bought the little man drinks he guzzled with gusto.

When the furor died down, the two moved on for repeat performances at McFadden's, Paddy O's, The Dubliner, Hurricane O'Reilly's, The Green Dragon, and J.J. Foley's.

Barely more than half over, the day already felt like the longest of Devin's life.

By NINE, Devin figured he was the only sober Irishman in town. And on St. Paddy's Day, every man was Irish.

He and Thomas were about to enter another pub when a familiar voice cut through the air.

"I should've known!" Megan rushed toward them, her flaming red hair matching her flushed cheeks.

Thomas blocked himself from Megan's view and tapped on Devin's knee. "We needs be going."

"Gimme just a minute."

Megan stopped in her tracks. "Who are you talking to?"

"I was..." Devin pointed to the spot next to his foot where—

Thomas was gone.

Devin looked about. "Where'd he go?"

"Who?"

"The, ah...did you see a little green man beside me?" Seeing the look on her face, he winced. "The...ah, leprechaun?"

Megan put her hands on her hips. "Devin Patrick, don't try that little green man stuff with me. I don't care how drunk you are."

"I haven't touched a drop. Honest."

She blinked.

"That's the point," Devin said. "He and I had a deal and now he's—"

"Who had a deal?"

"Me and the..." Devin looked away. "The leprechaun."

"Come on, Dev. What are you trying to—"

He grabbed her by the elbow. "Help me look inside."

Devin opened the door.

Megan drew in a deep breath. "What am I looking for?"

"A leprechaun."

She rolled her eyes. *"Oookaaay."*

Devin scanned the pub. "He and I had a deal."

"You sure you're not drunk?"

"That was the deal. I couldn't drink a drop the whole day. You know, St. Paddy's and all."

"But you're at a pub."

"That was the other part of the deal. I had to stay with him, watch him pound down one Guinness after another."

"The leprechaun."

"Yeah."

"He drank Guinness all day and you drank..."

"Diet Coke."

"I'm not sure which part is harder to believe."

They scoured the room, but Thomas was nowhere to be found.

"This isn't just a cock-and-bull story?"

"He promised me..." Devin rubbed his forehead. "A pot of gold. I know it sounds ridiculous, but...you should've seen him. He was standing right there." Devin felt like such a fool. "I wanted to do right by you. So I fell for it."

"And he had his fun until you looked away. Then he gave you the dodge."

Devin nodded glumly.

"That's your story?"

"Yeah."

Megan took his hand and led him to the bar. "Devin, my love, you need a drink."

TIFFANY GETS HER BOOBS

INTRODUCTION TO "TIFFANY GETS HER BOOBS"

This story came out of a Kris Rusch workshop assignment. We were to write a stand-alone story based on characters from something else we'd written, but the story had to work on its own. I thought of Tiffany, the Hooters waitress who becomes a sexy televangelist in my humorous novel *Bubba Goes for Broke*. She starts out as the secondary character, but bumps Bubba easily aside with a swing of her curvaceous hip.

Bubba doesn't stand a chance.

For the assignment, I decided to write Tiffany's story before the events of *Bubba Goes for Broke*. In the novel, she's already gotten her boob job and is poised for stardom.

"Tiffany Gets Her Boobs" describes how that boob job came to be.

As she did with "Little Blue Fuzzy," Kris graciously recommended "Tiffany" on her blog with words that warmed my heart.

"'Tiffany' works beautifully," Kris wrote, "and by the end of the story, I had fallen in love with this savvy, determined, and somewhat crazy woman. Everyone who has read this story remembers it and likes it. You will too."

You can only imagine the smile on my face when I read those words.

I electronically published the story with the hopes that it would convince readers to move on to the novel. Within a short time, I made the story free and it became a Top 100 free download.

But mostly for the wrong reasons.

I designed my own covers back then, and (cluelessly) figured a story about a woman getting a boob job required a well-endowed woman on the cover.

Yeah, I'm an idiot. Not quite as bad as in my teenage years when I was deciding Princeton was my number two school of choice because of a running back named Cosmo Iacavazzi (see the Introduction if you don't know what I'm talking about). But I'm frequently as much of an idiot now as I was all those decades ago.

Guys (and presumably girls who like girls) saw that cover and downloaded it with all the wrong expectations. "Tiffany Gets Her Boobs" became a Kindle bestselling free download and remained one for over two years, but it didn't generate many sales of *Bubba Goes for Broke*.

Surprise, surprise.

Fortunately, I eventually turned over my cover design to my awesome editor, Dayle Dermatis, and she pointed out (in far more gentle terms than I deserved) how the cover wasn't getting across the message I wanted.

Dayle designed new covers both for "Tiffany" and *Bubba*, with clear branding and art that linked them together. "Tiffany Gets Her Boobs" dropped off the free download bestseller list—no more horny guys downloading with the wrong expectations—but the story now serves its purpose as a fun story all by itself, and a sales pitch for *Bubba Goes for Broke.*

TIFFANY GETS HER BOOBS

Tiffany already had a pair. Just not a pair that she, or anybody else, liked.

Mosquito bites, that's what the girls in school had called them. They'd called her Tiffy Tiny Tits back then. The boys hadn't called her at all.

Even now, Tiffany remained as flat-chested as ever and figured if you didn't have boobs by the time you were eighteen, you weren't going to get them.

At least not the old-fashioned way.

She dreamed of becoming a star and having everyone admire her for her beauty. A star like Marilyn Monroe, whose posters adorned Tiffany's apartment walls; still a star almost fifty years after her death. Tiffany knew that she could have an otherwise cute figure and the platinum-blonde hair that bombshell stereotypes were made of, but stardom wasn't going to happen as long as she had a chest more like Jay-Z's than Beyoncé's.

Which was why she was mounting the steps to her brother Peter's house, a tiny two-bedroom with peeling white paint and a rotting front porch that sagged and creaked beneath her and smelled of mold and mildew. Peter didn't even own the house; he just lived there, in one of Boston's poorest suburbs. But Tiffany wasn't just a dreamer; she was a doer. And though the prospects seemed somewhere between slim and none, she figured the worst that could happen would be that he'd say no.

She put a smile on her face and rang the doorbell. Inside, an obnoxious loud buzz blared as if she'd just answered a question on *Jeopardy*. The tiny footfalls of a child sounded, followed by the louder steps of an adult.

A look of wary surprise crossed Peter's face. "Tiffany?" He lifted his two-year-old daughter, red-haired with freckles, into his arms. "What brings you here?"

Tiffany had done her homework. She waved at the little girl. "How's my little Rachel doing?"

Rachel shrunk away from her.

Tiffany smiled. "It's your Aunt Tiffany."

Rachel clung all the more fiercely to her father.

"She's shy," Peter said with a shrug. "Come on in."

The front room was barely larger than an oversized closet, furnished with a threadbare rug, a tattered chair, and a food-stained couch that must have been salvaged off the street on trash pickup day. The room smelled of diapers and baby powder. A picture of Jesus praying in the Garden of Gethsemane hung on the wall, concealing most of a dark stain on the faded wallpaper.

When Tiffany sat on the couch, a broken spring goosed her. She put her hands on her lap and forced a smile back onto her face. "So how's the preaching business going?"

"It's not a business," Peter said.

"Sorry, bad choice of words," she said, kicking herself for not preparing a script. "How are things going?"

Peter put Rachel on the floor. He leaned forward, resting

his forearms on his thighs. "Listen, I'm not crazy about you and you're not crazy about me. I wish you well and I pray for you often, but we're two different animals and let's not pretend otherwise. What brings you here?"

Tiffany drew in a deep breath. What had she been thinking? On a bad idea scale of one to ten, this was probably a thirteen.

"I was wondering if I could borrow some money," she said.

Peter stared at her. "Are you nuts?" He gestured to first one wall and the other. "Does it look to you like we have any extra money? We can barely keep up with the medicine and diapers for Rachel."

"I'd be able to pay you back really fast, I promise. If you could, like, take a cash advance on a credit card, I could pay you back with interest. It'll pay for itself."

"Do you know what my salary is?" Peter said, looking at her in disbelief. "There isn't a credit card company foolish enough to give us a line of credit. And if there were, we're not foolish enough to use it. We have to trust in the Lord, not Bank of America." He shook his head. "What have you gotten yourself into? And what do you mean, *It'll pay for itself*?"

A sour taste filled Tiffany's mouth. This was just going to result in ridicule, just like she expected. She licked her lips.

"It's for an operation."

Peter's eyebrows raised. "What's the matter? Are you all right?"

"I'm fine," Tiffany said. "Nothing's wrong with me." Seeing the concern on his face, she said, "Honest. This is elective surgery so it isn't covered by my health plan. That's all."

"Elective? What kind of elective?"

"If you can't help me, you can't help me. Let's leave it at that."

She got up to leave, but Peter reached out a hand to her.

"I can't help. We're broke. But I'm concerned. What kind of surgery?"

Tiffany smiled. "I need a boob job."

———

THE NEXT DAY, Tiffany dressed in her most conservative attire, a black, pinstriped, two-button business suit with matching pants, and headed for the Tri-County Credit Union in the Burlington Mall. She'd scolded herself after getting back to the apartment for subjecting herself to Peter's scorn until she finally convinced herself that she'd had few other options. It wasn't as though she was ever going to get in contact with Mother as long as Mother was with Creepy Charlie. So what if Peter humiliated her? She'd been getting humiliated one way or another all her life. Besides, what had it hurt other than her feelings for a couple hours? If nothing else, it had been a practice run for a more likely source of money.

Which was where the Tri-County Credit Union came in. Tiffany had her doubts—she was filled to overflowing with doubts—and felt more than a little sheepish about making such a brazen request, but didn't corporations do this kind of thing all the time? Why not her?

Besides, Marilyn Monroe hadn't become famous by hiding her light under a bushel, to use one of Peter's phrases. No, Marilyn Monroe had let that sucker shine, let it shine, let it shine.

It was time for Tiffany LeBlanc to do some shining.

She entered the credit union, a black purse in one hand

and a manila folder with her calculations in the other. The smells of the neighboring food court filled the air: Sbarro pizza, Taco Bell, d'Angelos subs, and of course, McDonalds. An older woman with graying hair sat behind the first desk and a dark-haired woman in her twenties sat behind the second. Tiffany recognized both of them from times she'd come in to cash her paycheck. She walked past them to the man seated behind the third desk, one with a nameplate that said Arthur L. Cromwell, Loans.

A short bald man with a bushy mustache and a disturbing amount of nose hair, Cromwell pointed to the chair opposite his pristinely clean desk.

"What can I do for you?"

Tiffany felt her resolve falter. What if he laughed at her? She'd been laughed at all through school, first for being the only girl so poor she wore patches on her clothes and then for being Tiffy Tiny Tits and never going to dances or getting asked out.

If this man—good God, that really was an obscene amount of nose hair—laughed at her, she'd feel just about ready to die.

Tiffany steeled herself for whatever might come and said, "I'd like a loan."

"Well, you've come to the right place." Cromwell grinned, showing nicotine-stained teeth. "What type of loan?" He opened his drawer. "There's a different form for each type." He chuckled. "They keep the vice presidents busy creating new forms every day." He chuckled some more at his superb wit.

"A medical loan," she said. "I need a loan for an operation."

"I see," Cromwell said gravely. "I'm sorry to hear that." He put both hands up a few inches off his desk in a defensive motion and said, "It's none of my business, but I hope it's nothing serious."

Tiffany smiled and told him that it wasn't. "It's really more of a business loan, the way I look at it."

Cromwell brightened. "That's good. We don't have a medical loan per se, but we certainly have business loans." He chuckled. "Plenty of forms for that." He grinned, inviting her to share his mirth.

She smiled back, trying not to look at the nose hairs. At the other desks, printers whirred and receipts were torn off and handed to customers.

"Like I said, I need an operation, one that isn't covered by my insurance," Tiffany said. "But it'll pay for itself in almost no time. That's why I'm saying it's really a business loan."

Confusion crossed Cromwell's face. "I'm not sure I understand. What type of operation, if I may ask."

Tiffany licked her lips and smiled. "A boob job."

Cromwell's jaw dropped. His eyes fell to her chest and then rocketed back up to her face. "Did I hear you correctly?"

Tiffany nodded. "I really want to be an actress. Or something like that. But..." She gestured toward her chest with both thumbs. "I think I need some help."

Cromwell wiped a bead of sweat off his forehead. He gulped. "I'm not sure if there's anything we can do for you. We'd be talking a personal loan and I'm not sure—"

"I keep my checking and savings account here," Tiffany said. "And you do loans. I figured you loan money to good customers, right?" Tiffany didn't believe her own bullshit, but she had to try. Marilyn might have had a few tough sales jobs herself.

Cromwell blinked. "Well, we do issue loans to good

customers," he said and chuckled nervously. "But it isn't that easy. Tell me, what is your account number?"

Tiffany rattled off the digits and Cromwell typed them into his computer.

"You have a little over a thousand dollars in savings," he said. "How much does a...um, a..." He glanced briefly down at her flat chest, apparently unable to say the word "boob." He cleared his throat. "How much of a loan are you looking for?"

"Six thousand dollars."

Beads of sweat formed again on Cromwell's forehead. He wiped them away. "Do you have anything you could use as collateral? A car? A house? Stocks?"

Tiffany shook her head. "But you said you have personal loans."

Cromwell pulled a chart out from his desk drawer. "What you're talking about is an unsecured loan. That's because you have no collateral." He pointed to a line on the chart. "The most we can offer anyone like yourself would be a three thousand dollar personal loan, contingent on a good credit report and solid earnings potential."

Tiffany pulled a sheet of paper out of her manila envelope. "Here's where I can make the operation pay for itself." She pointed to one row of figures. "This is how much I make working at The Gap." She pointed to a second row of figures. "This is how much I could make, tips included, working at the Hooters on Route 1."

Cromwell stared at her, seemingly unable to speak.

"I could pay the loan off with the difference in less than a year," she said. "Probably less than six months." She plunged on. "But I need six thousand dollars, not three thousand. Three would only get me one boob."

Cromwell just blinked.

"Forget the personal loan," Tiffany said. "I figure that this could be the safest business loan you ever give. It's a guaranteed return. If you need me to, I could form a corporation. Tiffany's Titties." She looked hopefully at Cromwell. When she got nothing but a blank stare, she said, "Or if that's too risqué for a corporation, how about Tiffany's Boobs?"

Cromwell finally broke out of his trance as a look of dawning recognition crossed his face. He leaned forward.

"Tell me truth," he said. "Where do you have the cameras?"

———

TIFFANY TRIED every bank and credit union in the area, sometimes wearing the same conservative garb and other times wearing her more sexy clothes to accentuate her true potential. But she struck out each time, except for with the two wolves who eyed her up and down and talked about a special kind of collateral. She got up and left quickly both of those times.

Which left her back in her studio apartment, staring at the three posters of Marilyn hanging on the wall behind the sofa: one, a headshot of Marilyn holding a pinkie to her sultry lips; another of her sitting down on stone steps, her black dress hiked up to expose fishnet stockings; and of course her most famous shot of all, the one with her standing on a subway grate, holding down her billowing skirt.

What would Marilyn do? Tiffany had no idea.

She soon began to despair that she'd ever get her boobs. She could barely pay the rent as it was. She wouldn't become the next Marilyn Monroe; she'd always be the one and only Tiffy Tiny Tits.

The idea came to her while drifting off to sleep on the couch with the TV on. She pulled the scratchy yellow blanket over herself, lay her head down on one of the couch's lumpy pillows, then shot bolt upright when a story made reference to runners in the upcoming Boston Marathon raising money for charity.

That was it! She had it! A fundraiser. Why hadn't she thought of it before?

She'd call it the *Boob-a-thon*.

———

SHE DIDN'T WANT to be too crass. A moderate amount of crassness was okay, even expected in someone seeking to become a Hooters girl, but she didn't want to go overboard. Too much of anything, whether crassness or even boobs, was a bad idea.

Tiffany figured a good balance would be a fifty-fifty split. She'd disperse half the funds for breast augmentation and the other half for breast cancer research. It could be an ongoing fundraiser. After she got her boob job, other worthy candidates could apply.

And it really wouldn't be taking money away from a worthy cause either. Horny guys—and weren't all guys horny?—would donate with big boobs in mind, but be able to tell themselves they'd given to a worthy cause. It'd be like the guys of past generations who'd bought *Playboy* magazine and said they were doing it to read the articles. It might not pass muster as a tax-exempt charity, but that was a detail she could look at later.

She wouldn't run twenty-six miles. She'd never be able

to do that; hell, she doubted she could *walk* twenty-six miles. But she figured she could walk half of that. She'd walk the first thirteen miles of the Boston marathon course before the procedure and the other half after. Donors would have to trust her and pay up front. And she'd deliver.

———

THE FENWAY PARK area buzzed with excitement. The New York Yankees were in town to take on the Red Sox. The smell of Italian Sausage, peppers, and onions was in the air. The greasy delicacy sizzled on the grill outside Gate B.

"Get your peanuts!" cried another vendor. "Get your red hot peanuts, pretzels, and Cracker Jacks."

Tiffany stood thirty yards away on the corner of Brookline Avenue and Yawkey Way, handing out her specially made handbills.

BOOB-A-THON, they proclaimed along the top. Running down from the two B's were the words Beautify and Boston. Along the bottom read, *Fight Breast Cancer*.

Tiffany held out the handbills, smiling and for the guys at least, trying to look cute, or at least as cute as she thought she could be pre-op. Most, however, passed right on by without taking the handbill, associating her with the kooks who were handing out political pamphlets or religious tracts that proclaimed, "Jesus Saves! Repent or burn in Hell!" Those in the sardine-packed crowd who took the handbills invariably tossed them to the ground five or six steps later.

In the twenty minutes before a tall, uniformed policeman told her to move along, she received seventeen propositions of varying levels of crudeness and a number of "accidental" hands brushing over her ass as they passed.

Glancing at the ground as she left, she saw the message to repent or go to hell and wondered if that message was for her. She probably deserved to burn in hell for what she was doing.

———

Tiffany came close to giving up until she realized she was going at the advertising the wrong way. Handbills? Forget it. How lame!

YouTube was the way to go. She tossed the first eleven attempts at a video in her PC's recycle bin, but thought she had the right mix of sexy flirtatiousness in the twelfth one. She didn't feel sexy, at least not yet. She was hoping that would come later. And she was no good at all with flirting, but this video at least had a shot.

She uploaded it and at first, nothing happened. Tiffany fell into a three-day funk, but emerged with one final last gasp attempt. After taking the subway into the city, she stopped at the first fraternity house on Commonwealth Avenue, one with a weathered brick exterior and a white wooden door.

She rang the doorbell and waited. No one came. She rang it again.

A pleasant-looking face with dripping wet hair poked out the door. "Yes?"

"Hi, my name is Tiffany," she said, her heart pounding as it did each time she tried her sales pitch. Her mouth felt dry and her hands unsteady. But she continued with her script. "I'm the organizer and an active participant for the First Annual Boob-a-Thon."

The boy looked about the shut the door until she got to the word *boob*. "What did you say?" he asked.

She described the fundraiser again.

"Can you come inside?" he asked.

Tiffany backed away. "No." That was the one thing she'd told herself she'd never do. She wasn't stepping foot alone inside any frat house no matter how good-looking the boy was who answered. "I have to stay out here. Sorry."

He laughed. "Then give me a second."

He took longer than two minutes. As Tiffany was about to leave, the boy opened the door and stepped out. About six feet tall and muscular. Green eyes, a nice smile, and a cast on his foot.

"Sorry, I was in the shower," he said. He pointed to the cast. "It takes me time to get around. I'm usually the last guy to answer the door, but everyone else is away at the intramural lacrosse match."

Tiffany smiled. "Sorry to bother you."

"No," he said, gesturing dismissively. "No bother. By the way, I'm Tyler and you said you were..."

"Tiffany."

When she explained the fundraiser, Tyler broke into a broad grin. "That's outstanding!" He laughed and shook his head. "You've got real balls and I mean that as a compliment." He ran his fingers through his wet hair. "This is perfect! Listen, I'll have to talk to the rest of the guys, but I'm the Social Chairman so I've got a lot of pull. If you're looking for a fraternity sponsor, you've got one. And I'll send an email to the rest of our chapters nationally and to some other houses we're close to. We'll get you your...enhancement before you know it."

WITHIN A WEEK, the YouTube video went viral. Two months

later, Tiffany completed the first thirteen miles of the challenge. A week later, she underwent the surgery.

Afterward, she looked at herself in the ceiling-to-floor mirror on the back of the bathroom door, posing at every angle and liking what she saw. She couldn't wait for her first high school reunion. She'd look up everyone who'd taunted her and get the last laugh. Payback would be a very snippy bitch.

But it wouldn't end there. This wasn't about revenge for the past. This was for the future. She walked out to stand before the Marilyn Monroe posters on the wall, focusing on Marilyn and her billowing skirts above the subway grate.

"I'm going to be a star," Tiffany said, pointing at Marilyn. "Just wait and see."

ONE-NIGHT STANDS FOR
LOVE AND GLORY

INTRODUCTION TO "ONE-NIGHT STANDS FOR LOVE AND GLORY"

And so we come to the final story. We've gone from female impersonators to the Old Testament to many oddball stops in between. Thank you for sharing this journey with me.

Now we go to outer space.

If you're not a science fiction fan, please give the story a chance. There isn't much science in the story. It's really all about the heart.

As I believe the best stories almost always are.

"One-Night Stands for Love and Glory" will make you laugh, and it will make you cry.

ONE-NIGHT STANDS FOR LOVE
AND GLORY

Now where was I?

Oh, yes, of course. The introduction. How silly of me.

Welcome to the show, ladies and gentlemen. What a great crowd we have here in the...the, um...what is the name of this place?

Yes! Yes, thank you. The People's Auditorium. Of course. I knew that. I was just testing you, ha ha.

It's a delight to be here. It's been a long time since I performed under a straw thatch roof. And the gaps in the logs that make up these walls provide such wonderful ventilation. What a good thing that is. I can tell most of you were working really hard in the fields today. Smells like some of you might even have been spreading manure, ha ha.

I'm just joking. You're a great audience. Give yourself a hand!

Get on with the show?

Ah, yes. A splendid idea. Splendid!

There's just one problem. As you may have surmised, I'm stalling. I tell you that in a spirit of forthright openness.

No, there's no reason for you to leave. And there are positively no refunds! Of course not, the show is free, ha ha.

Please be patient. I'm experiencing technical difficulties. My AI is not responding.

Yes, a chip implant translates my words into your local dialect, but I need Artie, my AI, to translate them even further into your culture. Most jokes make no sense without the correct cultural grounding. I really can't start without him.

Artie?

Folks, please sit down. This is temporary, I assure you. He'll be with us momentarily.

One Universal Credit to everyone who stays for the entire show! You have my word on it. Your patience will be rewarded.

Hey, there's no need to throw anything.

Oooh. That one was juicy. Really now! That was quite unnecessary.

Oh my, that one was rotten.

Two credits to everyone who stays! Without, of course, throwing either soft rotten objects or very hard ones.

Ah, that's more like it. You are a fine and cultured audience.

Artie? Artieeeeeee?

Let me demonstrate, folks why I can't perform without my AI. You might even find this enlightening.

As the old phrase goes, please stand by.

You're sitting down.

Why are you still sitting down? This is where I'm supposed to tell you that "Please stand by" is only a phrase, a figure of speech, not meant to be taken literally. A phrase that Artie would have translated into one that you understood.

But you did understand. How did you do that?

Artie? You're here? What do you mean you've been here all along?

Ah, well, let's get on with the show then.

Folks, I flew in just last night and boy, are my arms tired.

————

I'm glad that one is over. I thought the crowd was going to lynch me there for a while. But they came around after a while, the bunch of dumb hicks. Not all the way, but enough for me to see their front teeth, all two or three of them, as they laughed. The front row looked like a picket fence.

At least a few of the jokes scored. Not as many as in the old days when Artie was in his prime, but enough.

Now where was I? What was I saying?

Oh yes, Artie.

He's slipping, bit by bit, byte by byte. It's sad, not just for him but for me, too, because I can't make it without him. When he's gone—gone for good, I mean, not just gone for a while like now—I'll be nothing.

Of course, I'm pretty close to nothing even with him. If I were *something*, I'd be in one of the galactic centers, where all the great comic talents showcase their brilliance. I tried that for a time, crashed and burned, so now I play these two-bit halls out here in the Great In-Between, where habitable planets are few and far between and comic brilliance can't be found.

On Old Earth, they said of New York City that if you could make it there, you could make it anywhere. Out here in the cosmic boonies, we say that if you *can't* make it anywhere, you try the Great In-Between.

That's my joke, by the way. I steal most of my material,

but that's an Earl Weatherbee original. If you liked it, come to my next show and drop a Universal Credit in the hat on your way out.

I could get another AI, of course, but Artie and I have been working together so long—over fifty years—I could never adjust. And if I could, I doubt it would be worth it. No other AI could match his old brilliance. Your average AI can make the translation when there's a one-to-one match in the cultures. But Artie, before he started this slide, could pull off even the most impossible of matches.

Don't believe me?

Well, let me tell you about the joke that started it all and you can be the judge.

———

WHEN I WAS TWELVE, my best friend, Jimmy Chiasson, and I were Old Earth history buffs. These days, I can take it or leave it but back then both of us were addicted. We loved to go into the archives and relive Old Earth history, playing all sorts of strange recordings, things they called "movies" and "TV shows" back then.

Jimmy and I watched and listened to them all, but for one brief stretch we liked the Lone Ranger TV show best of all. We got a chill up and down our spines just hearing the theme music. It went like this: *tada-dum, tada-dum, tada-dum-dum-dum. Tada-dum, tada-dum, tada-dum-dum-dum.*

That theme song gave birth to my first joke ever and sent me on to a life of one-night stands. I'm almost certain I made it up myself—who could I have stolen it from?—but you know how it is with us low-rent comics; we've stolen so many jokes, we can't recall what's really our own and what's somebody else's bastard child.

Now where was I? Bastard child...um, oh yeah. Where it all started. Sorry. If I didn't know better, I'd think that whatever Artie has is catchy and I've lost a few of my own marbles. But that's ludicrous. I know I've still got it.

Anyways, back then I was as horny as any other boy my age, so one time, for some reason I'll never understand, I happened to think of naked women at the same time the Lone Ranger theme song came on.

Tada-dum, tada-dum, tada-dum-dum-dum.

I had a burst of comic inspiration. I paused the recording and turned to Jimmy.

"If you had a room of a hundred naked women," I said, catching his attention right away. "And they all laid down on the floor, one face up and then the next face down, one face up, and the next face down...how would that be like the Lone Ranger?"

Jimmy grinned. "I don't know."

"*Titty-bum, titty-bum, titty-bum-bum-bum.*"

Jimmy howled with laughter. He laughed so hard he had to hold his sides.

I was hooked. I knew what I wanted to do with my life. What I *had* to do for the rest of my life. I had to make people laugh like that every day.

Some days I want to damn Jimmy's soul to Hell for that laughter, for those tears that trickled down the sides of his face. If he'd only given me a frown and called me a stupid pervert, he'd have spared me the life I've lived, hopping about in the Great In-Between, having to pay people not to leave my shows.

I can't even say that it's a living. Not that I need one. My parents left me a trust fund so huge not even I could possibly squander it. I get my gigs only by agreeing to appear without compensation, paying all my own interstellar expenses.

Which means I'm the saddest of all artists. I don't do it for the money. I do it for the love. And you know what that means.

I'm not good enough for anyone to pay me.

———

So where was I?

Oh, yeah. Artie losing it.

No, that isn't right.

Where the Hell was I?

Oh yeah, Artie's old brilliance and the Lone Ranger joke. That's it.

You see, that's about as cultural as any joke you're ever going to hear. It doesn't make any sense unless you know the Lone Ranger theme song. And what percentage of the human population, especially out here in the galactic boondocks, knows that? Virtually zero. Plus, the local people need to have words in their dialect for their titties and bums that match the words you'd use for the rhythms of that music.

The odds are astronomical.

And yet, I include that joke in every show. It's my signature joke in fact, and somehow Artie's been able to translate it every time and it always brings down the house.

Well, maybe it doesn't bring down the house. I don't ever really *bring down the house.* But the joke works. Every time. One of the best in my repertoire.

Until recently, of course. Until Artie began to drop a few bits here and there. Then a few more.

Now, as a team we're in crisis mode. He acts as though

it's me that's messing up. He can't accept the fact that I'm sharp as ever and it's him that's losing it and losing it fast.

It's so sad.

The denial must be an AI thing.

———

It got worse on the next planet. But it turned out great in its own way.

Artie bombed, leaving me dying up there on stage.

Dying, I tell you.

I went five minutes without a laugh and then ten. I had expected the hillbilly audience of about five hundred to be easy picking, as willing as a horny ninety-year-old man to take whatever entertainment it could get.

But by the fifteen-minute mark, the frozen smiles were long gone. I'd coaxed not a single laugh out of any of them. Men and women looked at each other confused. A man in the front row turned to what I assume was his wife and mouthed the words, "This is comedy?"

I knew then that Artie, who'd been slipping, had lost it for good. My material was the same as always, but Artie's translations were missing the mark.

As people shifted uncomfortably in their seats, long past the twenty-minute mark, I was rescued only in the most bizarre and humiliating of ways.

Suddenly, a peach-faced young man in the very middle of the audience stood up and yelled, "He's a Kaufmanite!" He spread his arms wide and grinned broadly. "Like the comedian on Old Earth. He's *trying* to be bad! That's what's so funny!"

And he howled with laughter.

As bad as the twenty minutes of dead silence had been, this was worse. Far worse. It was a mocking slap in the face.

But a few people around him began to titter and then as he continued to roar and slap his leg, so did they. Couples looked at each other, first confused and then with dawning amusement. The laughter became infectious, spreading out from the young man like ripples in the water after a stone has been tossed into it.

Soon the entire auditorium was howling and slapping their legs. Some of them in the front row were laughing so hard, they were crying.

When they broke into thunderous applause, I almost said, "I'm not done, I've got lots more where that came from."

But I thought better of it.

I spread my arms wide and bowed.

"You're too kind," I mouthed to them. I blew them kisses. As the cheering reached its crescendo, I bowed again.

And walked off the stage to the first standing ovation of my career.

———

I SHOULD HAVE CALLED it quits right then. Gone out on a high note. A standing ovation after the last performance of my career! Yes, the truth would have mocked me. The laughter and applause for all the wrong reasons would have haunted my days and nights.

But I might have become a legend out here in the Great In-Between. The two-bit comic with a brief flash of brilliance, showing his true genius in that one singular bravura performance. Knowing he could never duplicate it, he retired atop the very peak of the comic mountaintop. The most romantic of all artistic legends short of also blowing my brains out.

Legends, after all, are created easily out here in the galactic boonies because the fabric they require is so scarce and the hunger for them is so fierce.

That outcome might have been the funniest joke of all, even funnier than the one about the Lone Ranger.

Earl Weatherbee, legendary comic.

A *real* knee-slapper.

But I'm a creature of habit. Moving from planet to planet and solar system to solar system is what I do. Besides, I'd have probably blabbed the truth on my deathbed and ruined the romantic legend anyway.

So I moved on to the next one-night stand and the one after that and eventually took the stage on a planet with two rival humanoid races, one with traditional arms and legs, the Bipeds, and the other with eight tentacled appendages, the Octoids.

An aisle ran through the middle of the auditorium—there was not a single center seat—and the two races sat on their respective sides. Artie couldn't reach out to two such contradictory cultures, even though he'd mastered even that impossible task in his prime. That feat was beyond him now.

So, of course, I bombed.

He bombed, but *I* was the one left standing in front of the crowd with an embarrassed grin on my face. Undressed, in a manner of speaking.

Less than halfway through the show, the crowds streamed to their respective exits, members of both races equally unwilling to subject themselves to the performance even when offered five Universal Credits apiece.

———

I WAITED until I was back in the hotel room with its rusted sink, leaky faucet, and squeaking bed. Damp moldy smells filled my nostrils. The bitter, almost sour aftertaste of the local malt beverage clung to my palate.

I'd been in this place, or places like it, my entire adult life. But no more.

"Artie, we have to talk," I said out loud.

You don't have to shout, he replied.

"I'm not shouting."

It feels like it.

For the longest time, we'd communicated almost subconsciously. I'd *thought* the words and he'd received them, replying in kind. But words of this import— words of beginnings, words of endings—demanded more.

"I need to say this out loud. For me, if not for you."

Knock yourself out.

"I don't know if you've noticed the audience reactions lately."

How could I not? I may not be organic, but your senses are mine.

I nodded. "We've been dying lately."

We?

Relief washed over me. Artie knew and was accepting the blame. I wouldn't have to spell it out for him. Yet with that relief came a sudden onrushing wave of sadness.

Could there be a more tragic plight than that of a once brilliant consciousness, whether organic or AI, reduced first to mediocrity and then to a barely aware feeblemindedness?

"I'm so very sorry."

You're doing the best you can.

"I'll never trade you—" I stopped. "What did you just say?"

Don't feel badly. I know you're trying as hard as you can.

"But..." I cocked my head. "I'm not the problem."

Who is?

Silence hung in the air for what felt like forever.

"You don't think..."

You can't possibly think—

"I'm telling the same jokes as always."

Are you?

"Of course. I haven't written or stolen a new joke in years."

But you aren't telling them anymore. Most of the time you're just babbling gibberish. It's untranslatable. I love a challenge, but I can't turn random babbling into a local joke. I can only turn it into locally understood random babbling. You're giving me nothing to work with.

"Random babbling? You call my act random babbling?"

That's what it is. Babbling about the cutie in row seven or the foul smell of the air or how you hate Jimmy Chiasson.

"I said that?"

Check the diagnostic logs. They'll show your input and my output.

My head felt light. The hotel room with its water-stained walls and dank smells spun all about me. "Garbage in, garbage out?"

You said it, not me. Or you tell the same joke in the same performance.

"I do not!"

Three times tonight. Would you like me to tell you which ones?

I shook my head, unable to speak.

Or you get halfway through a joke, then forget the punch

line. You stand there and I can't help you. You just start it all over again. Sometimes you get stuck in a loop like that, repeating the first half over and over.

"I do?"

The worst one tonight lasted over five minutes.

"Five minutes?"

I suddenly recalled all the times I'd stood before a full auditorium, unable to remember why I was there. A cold chill crept up and down my spine.

"I'm losing it...aren't I?"

Some things are still clear for you. You've never forgotten the Lone Ranger joke. But I have to be honest.... Yes, you're losing it. I'm so very sorry.

My heart thudded and my palms felt moist. "Can't you... I mean, you know my material by heart, why don't you fix it when I start...when I start losing it?"

You don't know the answer? I thought sure you would remember that.

"The answer to what?"

To why I can't override you.

"Override me when?"

Do you see what I mean?

"No, I don't see." I blinked my eyes and licked my lips. "What were we talking about?"

About me overriding you.

"I forbid it! I'm the maestro. You are but the instrument!"

Exactly.

"Exactly what?"

We were talking about your fugues.

"We were? What fugues?"

And how I'm powerless to help you when they happen on stage.

"You are?"

They're happening almost all the time now, but you've forbidden me to help.

Clouds parted within my mind.

"You're serious? I've really lost it?"

I'm afraid so. It's getting worse and worse.

"Lost and gone forever? Dreadful sorry, Clementine?"

Dreadful sorry, Earl.

"This is awful. What will I do? What will *you* do?"

Don't worry. I won't leave you. I'll stay with you, no matter what.

"Until...until the very..."

I couldn't speak that last word.

Yes.

"You shouldn't."

Try to stop me.

I thought of all our years together. Good times. Bad times. I'd never expected it to end like this.

"I don't want to stop performing." I bowed my head. "But if I'm just humiliating myself..."

Let me help. I know the material. When you space out, I'll take over. We'll be co-maestros.

"You think so?"

You could maybe even try some new material. I've thought up some for you.

"Use your material?"

Only if you want to.

———

AT OUR NEXT SHOW, we killed them. The audience, I mean. Perhaps a modest success by inner galactic standards, but a rip-roaring smash out here in the Great In-Between.

Artie's new material about having sex with an Octoid woman got some of the biggest laughs.

Women with tentacles, woo-ee, they'll grab your scrawny ass, never let go, and have six limbs left over for everything else!

For the first time in decades, I found myself laughing. Not fake stage laughter. But really laughing.

"Knock 'em dead, Artie," I whispered. "Knock 'em dead."

HE'S DOING MORE and more of each show. Not that Artie's taking over or anything like that. Just that my blank spots are becoming more and more frequent. I'm leaning more and more heavily on him all the time. We both know the old Earl Weatherbee isn't coming back.

You wouldn't believe how long I had to wait just to clearly tell you these few words.

But I'm not going to quit. Making people laugh is my life. It's who I am; it's what I do. If I need a little help—or a lot of help—so what?

It doesn't matter which one of us is telling the jokes, does it? Who cares? Artie and me, we're a team. I've hopped on his back and he's carrying me home. It's a nice back. A hell of a back.

And if he's all I have as the last of my flickering lights go out...well, that's all right with me.

ACKNOWLEDGEMENTS

To Kris Rusch, Dean Wesley Smith, and Jeanne Cavelos for all the reasons I described in this book's introduction. Your instruction has meant the world to me.

To my editor, Dayle Dermatis, whose expertise saves me from myself time after time.

To all my family and friends who have supported me and helped me share the joy of laughter.

I love you all.

ALSO BY DAVID H. HENDRICKSON

Novels

Bubba Goes for Broke

Cracking the Ice

Offside

Offensive Foul

Short Stories

Blue Note Heaven

All Over Again

Feline Masterpiece

Drawing Dead

My Dark Angel

Baby, One More Time

Beloved

Writing as D. H. Hendrickson

(Hockey Romance)

Novels

Body Check

No Defense

Short Stories

Shooting for the Moon

David H. Hendrickson's first novel, *Cracking the Ice*, was praised by Booklist as "a gripping account of a courageous young man rising above evil." He has since published five additional novels, including *Offside*, which has been adopted for high school student required reading, and most recently, *Offensive Foul*.

His short fiction has appeared in *Ellery Queen's Mystery Magazine*, *Heart's Kiss*, *Pulphouse*, and numerous anthologies, including over a half dozen issues of *Fiction River*. His story "Death in the Serengeti," won the 2018 Derringer Award for Best Long Story, and was also selected for *Best American Mystery Stories 2018*.

Hendrickson has published over fifteen hundred works of nonfiction, most recently his first book for writers, *How to Get Your Book into Schools and Double Your Income with Volume Sales*, and also *Travis Roy: Quadriplegia and a Life of Purpose*. He has been honored with the Joe Concannon Hockey East Media Award and the Murray Kramer Scarlet Quill Award.

Get a free short story and be notified of new releases by signing up for his mailing list at www.hendricksonwriter.com.

A Special Request from the Author: Word of mouth is crucial for any author to succeed. If you enjoyed this book, please consider leaving a review where you purchased it. Even if it's only a line or two, it would make all the difference and would be very much appreciated.

For more information
www.hendricksonwriter.com/
david@hendricksonwriter.com